Children of the Second Morning

~ *Tales of Karensa* ~

Jean Cullop

Scripture Union

By the same author

Tales of Karensa: Where Dolphins race with Rainbows
Tales of Karensa: Castle of Shadows
Tales of Karensa: Silver Serpent, Golden Sword

Copyright © Jean Cullop
First published 2001
Reprinted 2002

Scripture Union, 207–209 Queensway, Bletchley,
Milton Keynes, MK2 2EB, England.
Email: info@scriptureunion.org.uk
Website: www.scriptureunion.org.uk

ISBN 1 85999 526 8

British Library Cataloguing-in-Publication Data.
A catalogue record of this book is available from the British
Library.

Printed and bound in Great Britain by Creative Print and
Design (Wales) Ebbw Vale.

Scripture Union is an international Christian charity working
with churches in more than 130 countries, providing
resources to bring the good news about Jesus Christ to
children, young people and families and to encourage them
to develop spiritually through the Bible and prayer.

As well as our network of volunteers, staff and associates
who run holidays, church-based events and school Christian
groups, we produce a wide range of publications and
support those who use our resources through training
programmes.

Contents

Karensa

The Lost Kingdom

As far away as yesterday is an island called Karensa, where dolphins race with rainbows and woodland creatures walk freely in the Dark Forest, and broken hearts are healed.

The people of Karensa had lived and spoken in ways unchanging since ancient times and each one could go to the King, who met every need with perfect love and justice.

Then came the Day of Sorrow when Lord Bellum disobeyed the King and for that he was cast out of the Royal Palace. Fear was born on Karensa, and the way to the King was closed. Lord Bellum built his own castle, for he was determined that one day he, not the King, would be ruler of Karensa, and many people believed the false promises he made.

The King's word decreed that the punishment for disobedience was death, and the King would not put his own desires above the truth of his word. His people must die.

Yet this King loved his people more than they would ever know, and in love sent his son, Salvis, to die in their place, although his own heart was broken.

So it was at the very moment Salvis died, all those who were held captive in Bellum's castle were set free and defeat was turned into a great victory.

Salvis now lives again in the Royal Palace and to all who put their trust in him, he gives forgiveness and the King's power. This means that the people may once again approach the King, who will hear them call even from the silence of their hearts.

So it will be on Karensa until the day that Salvis rides out from the Palace and claims back the Lost Kingdom.

The Children's Song

The Children of the Second Morning,
Awaiting the New Day's dawning.

Children against the night,
Seeking the Spirit's light.
Children prepared to fight,
Standing for truth and right.

We're the Children of the Second Morning,
Hearts ready for the New Day's dawning.

Chapter 1

"Who are you really?"

It was Christmas Eve, and snowing. Now that he had reached the small park above the town, Luke unclipped the dog's lead and the little collie raced off, completely snow-crazy.

Named Pepper for the way her black coat was sprinkled with white, she was hardly more than a puppy, and this was the first time she had seen snow. She barked at it, snuffled it with her nose, rolled in it, ate it, then chased her own tail, sending showers of white everywhere.

Luke laughed and threw some snowballs for her to catch. She tried to kill them and growled at them when they fell apart, then she ran off, dragging what looked like half a tree across the park. Luke left her to play on her own.

He went over to the stone wall surrounding the park and looked down to Poldawn. He should have been in church with Dad and Dad's wife, Stacey, and Rosie, Luke's ten-year-old sister. Everyone was going carol singing afterwards to raise money for charity.

Rosie had tried to encourage him.

"Come on, Luke, it's only once a year and it's for a good cause. How would you like to be homeless in this weather?"

"Someone's got to take Pepper for a walk," he

had answered stubbornly.

"You mean you don't want to go to church. You'd sooner be out in the snow," she snapped. Once, Rosie had been scared of her brother's moods, but not any more. Luke was calmer now and Rosie was learning not to be afraid.

Things had changed since Luke and Rosie had returned from Karensa, the strange island where the dolphins had taken them last summer and where they had lived for almost a year.

Luke and Rosie had changed. The family had changed. Now they all belonged to the small chapel in Poldawn and they had all made new friends.

"So? What if I do want to go out in the snow? It could be gone tomorrow and then Pepper will miss it!"

"No she won't! There must be two metres of snow out there and the weatherman said there's more to come. The snow will be around for at least a week."

"It might not be. Anyway..."

"Anyway, what?"

Luke didn't reply.

Anyway, he thought, strange things are happening to my voice and I can't sing properly.

Anyway, he was fed up with church. He was getting bored. The chapel was really lively, with its own youth group, but even so, he was bored! Stand up, sit down, sing the same chorus ten times, listen to the minister spouting on about sin and all the things you shouldn't do, and then get down on your knees and talk to someone who wasn't there! No, thank you very much.

Anyway, Luke had better things to do with his

time: playing rugby, bike riding, rowing along the creek, surfing or just being with his friends.

There were lots of things Luke didn't like these days. Being indoors by ten o'clock was one of them. Taking his friends home was another. Stacey always made them welcome, but she spoke openly about her faith. Luke's friends liked her and she never tried to force her ideas on them, but Luke was embarrassed. Besides, the whole house needed decorating. Their sofa sagged and squeaked, and Pepper had chewed a hole in the hall rug. Luke's friends had modern homes with bright, new furniture and the latest TVs. Compared to their houses, Luke's looked tacky! It was so old-fashioned.

Anyway, none of his friends went to church, so why should he be different? He had tried to get them to go with him, but they had laughed and refused, looking at him as though they felt sorry for him.

It had been different on the island...

Luke pulled his woollen hat down over his fair hair. It had stopped snowing at last but it was very cold. People were saying they had not seen so much snow for years.

"I remember back in 1963," or "If you'd been here in 1947," older people were saying, and Luke would groan and think, Here we go again. It's you who don't know what a real winter's like. If only you did know. If only you'd seen the snow on the island...

As he stood there in the park, memories flooded back, and he quickly pushed them away. That part of his life was over. In spite of this, or maybe because of it, he slipped his hand inside his fleece. He could still feel the scar on his shoulder where he had been injured on a day just like this, on the island of Karensa.

With the memories came a long-lost thudding of his heart and almost before he knew it, he had whispered under his breath, "Salvis, where are you now? I miss you! I can't find you any more!"

His words were lost in the falling snow but that did not stop the memories. Karensa and the people he had learnt to care so much about: Petroc, Morwen, the unforgettable Salvis, the King's son who had given up his own life for his people. There was no-one ever like Salvis.

Luke made a great effort and switched his thoughts to Christmas Day tomorrow and the presents he would be getting. At least they were real. Karensa seemed like a dream, only that scar on his shoulder told him Karensa was no dream.

As he stood by the wall, cold and lost in thought, he suddenly became aware of a man standing by his side.

He called Pepper, but there was no need because the little collie was sitting quietly at the man's feet. That was unusual. Pepper was too friendly and hadn't yet learnt it was wrong to jump up.

The man nodded. "That's a fine dog you have there, boy," he said, and his voice reminded Luke of someone, but he couldn't think who it was.

"She's only ten months old," he replied. "We got her last summer, when... after... me and my sister, we'd been away for a time."

"Yes," the man agreed. "So you had."

It was an odd reply. Luke didn't know what to say to it, so he said nothing.

"Are you training her?" the man asked.

"Pepper? We will be, after Christmas. She won't need much training, though. She's a good dog."

"Collies are easy to train," the man agreed, then he added, "So, Luke, how have you been?"

Luke had not told the stranger his name. How did he know who he was?

"OK... I suppose..." Then, without understanding why he said it, he blurted out, "The rest of the family are in church."

"So why not you?"

"I don't know... I... I get bored..."

The stranger nodded wisely. "You need to find the door, Luke, the door that only you can unlock."

All at once, Luke's heart was beating very fast. There was something so familiar about this man. Luke stared at him. He was tall and slim and had light brown hair and kind eyes, but Luke did not think he had ever seen him before, or if he had, he could not remember where it was.

"Who are you?" he asked. "Who are you really?"

The man smiled sadly. "Oh Luke, the last time you asked me that we were in a cave. You know who I am, don't you? I once promised I would always live in your heart. I promised I would never leave you or forsake you. And I have kept my promise. I have not left you, Luke. You have left me."

"Salvis?" Luke whispered wonderingly. "Salvis, is it you? Is it really you?"

Pepper chose that very moment to bark, which

distracted Luke, and when he looked up, the man had gone. The only footprints in the snow were his own.

Luke knelt down and threw his arms around Pepper, burying his face in her soft fur. He was shaken and confused. Was the man really Salvis? Or was it just his own imagination? How could Salvis have left Karensa and come here, to Cornwall?

Luke had left it too late to find the answers to his questions. Salvis had gone. Only his words remained.

"I will never leave you or forsake you... You have left me... Luke, find the door, the door only you can unlock..."

Salvis was calling him back.

Chapter 2
A gentle, friendly land

Far away from Poldawn, on the island of Karensa, two figures trudged through the snow. After leaving Petroc's farm at dawn and walking for several hours through the Dark Forest, they had come to a place where the road dwindled to a narrow woodland track. Here the snow was unmarked and the path overgrown on either side by frosty brambles and nettles.

The man and the boy were dressed in loose-fitting trousers, long belted tunics and high boots. Around their shoulders were cloaks of fur to keep out the intense cold, for the Time of Snows on Karensa was very harsh.

They both had shoulder-length fair hair and the man's hair was heavily streaked with grey. Both had thin faces and sharp features and both carried their belongings wrapped in bundles over their shoulders. They could easily have been father and son, but they were not. The man's name was Carrik and the boy was his nephew, Esram.

At fourteen years old, Esram had plenty of energy and could have walked on for several miles, but he saw that his uncle was in need of a rest.

They were on the very edge of the Dark Forest. Before them, in the distance, were the high moors which they would have to cross to reach their destination on the far side of the island. To their right, across the valley called the Meadow of Flowers, towered the dark, forbidding castle of the King's enemy, Lord Bellum. Many feared this castle, but those people still loyal to the King had been given power and knew that Bellum could not stand against them.

Esram pointed to a fallen log. "We could rest here, Uncle."

"We have food to eat and milk fresh this morning from the goat," Carrik agreed, and spread his cloak on the log, thankful to sit down.

At first they ate in silence, too hungry to speak. They could not help looking over to the distant castle where once Carrik had been Lord Bellum's highest servant. It seemed the more people who joined Bellum, the darker and bigger his castle became, so there would always be enough room.

Esram's thoughts were confused. Not long ago he had lived in that castle. He had worn fine clothes and feasted on rich food and wine. He had been Lord Esram, and servants ran to his command. Esram had loved to command!

Then one day he had met a simple farm girl called Morwen, who was a prisoner in the castle. Morwen had shown him the meaning of friendship, loyalty and love. She helped him turn away from Lord Bellum to Salvis, and now, for the first time in his life, he knew the meaning of happiness.

Esram had rescued Morwen from the castle and gone to live on her brother Petroc's farm.

The next day, Carrik had arrived at the farm to destroy it, but instead he, too, had joined the King's service, and his cruelty and greed were gone for ever.

Now they were on their way to the far side of the island to win back the people there for the King.

Carrik saw him looking at the castle. "Would you go back there, Esram?" he asked gently. Even Carrik's voice had changed. The mocking tones and the harshness were gone.

"No, never." Esram shook his head. "I could never go back there. I hate the person I used to be. What of you, Uncle?"

"We are changed now," Carrik replied. "We were both cruel and selfish then. We should not gaze at that castle. Come, nephew, we must go now if we are to reach the safety of the far side of the island before dark."

He had no desire to meet Lord Bellum, who had sworn to kill them both for betraying him.

Neither he nor Esram knew that Lord Bellum was watching them from the secrecy of the Dark Forest.

As they walked on together, they spoke of the task the King had set them.

Esram had doubts. "I never really met Salvis, not when he lived with the island people, Uncle Carrik, so how shall I be able to tell others about someone I never knew?"

"The King will show you the way. He will help us. We have to trust him. He would not ask us to do this and then leave us alone."

They continued in silence, and although they had left Petroc's farm in deep snow, the weather began to change as they neared the high moors. It grew warmer, so they threw off their cloaks. By the time they started to climb up to the moors, the snow was patchy, but when they reached the highest point, it began to rain heavily. Then Esram saw the barn.

"Look, Uncle, that barn seems empty. We can shelter in there until the rain stops. It will soon pass."

"I hope so, boy," Carrik said grimly. "My tunic is already soaked. I never saw such rain! This seems a miserable place and I hope it is not all so bleak as this moor!"

"It will not be, I'm sure. Petroc said it was a kind land. He would not lie to –"

Esram's words froze on his lips and his legs started to shake as three horsemen rode into the barn. The men were dressed as soldiers in grey tunics and dark blue cloaks, and each had a sword at his side. Esram hoped no-one noticed that he was scared. He had seen his friend Petroc face danger without once betraying fear. Esram wanted to be like Petroc.

They filled the barn, but the soldiers did not attempt to dismount. They sat on their horses and looked down on Esram and his uncle. The leader was a big, handsome man, with hair the colour of corn. He was dressed like the others except for a heavy gold chain around his neck.

"Greetings, friends. I am Tomas, leader of the Guardians. You are strangers here. May I ask your business?"

His voice was friendly enough, but there was something about him that Esram did not trust. He could not explain what it was.

"We come in peace to bring peace," was Carrik's reply.

"Peace? We have peace! We live in peace with

one another, each giving help to the other when it is needed."

"There is another peace," Carrik explained. "There is the deep peace of the heart that only the King can give."

At the mention of the King, Tomas became annoyed.

"We do not serve that King any more," he said curtly. "That King has closed the way to his palace so we may not go there any more. Why should we serve him? We have formed our own government called the Guardians and it is I, Tomas, whom the people depend on now. I meet their needs, not the King, nor his dead son, either!"

"Salvis is not dead," Carrik said quietly. "He was dead, but he now lives for ever in the Royal Palace. And what of the needs of an empty heart? Can you meet those needs? Ah, Tomas, my friend, I too deserted the King. I was Salvis' worst enemy and hated his followers. Yet I have turned back to him! The King's way is the right way to live!"

There was a short silence, and the men seemed to be considering what he had said. Then Tomas threw back his head and laughed. It was the last thing Esram and Carrik expected to hear.

"Well, I am pleased for you," Tomas said in between shouts of laughter. "But I must tell you, the people in these parts are quite happy with their life as it is. They are cared for by my men and they receive justice. They will not be interested in Salvis or in the King."

"We shall see," Carrik replied, still in that same calm voice.

Esram spoke for the first time. "It has stopped

raining now," he said, hoping the Guardians would go.

"So it has," Tomas agreed. "We must leave you, my friends. Welcome to our town, but remember my words. My people will not want to hear what you have to say. They do not want to go back to the King's law."

The three horsemen rode away, leaving Esram and Carrik standing in the empty barn. They were on the edge of the moor, where the ground fell away steeply and the land below them was hidden by mist.

As they walked outside, the sun came out and the mist cleared, revealing a most beautiful country of rolling hills, vineyards, orchards and green pastures; a gentle, friendly land. Basking in the sunlight was a town of white-walled houses and beyond that, the sea.

"No-one said it would be easy," Carrik replied to Esram's unspoken doubts. "Come then, Esram, let us go to the town. We shall need somewhere to stay this night. I feel we should look first for a man of peace who will receive us."

As they began the steep descent from the moors, a familiar figure rode off in the opposite direction, a tall, dark-haired man seated on a black horse and with a sword of black steel at his side.

Lord Bellum sped back towards his castle, his face ashen and his dark eyes glinting with amber, as they always did when he was angry.

Chapter 3

"We have no king nor lord"

He was a small, round sort of man, with bright blue eyes, brown hair and rosy cheeks. He was dressed from head to foot in green and he stood outside the door of a boot-maker's shop. Esram liked him at once.

Everyone was so kind here that Esram wondered why he had been afraid. The town was so neat! The white-walled houses each had a tub of flowers outside the door. Even the cobbles beneath their feet had been swept and doorsteps were scrubbed clean.

Shops were bright and colourful. The baker's displayed trays of cakes filled with cream. Another shop sold tunics of every colour; another red, shiny apples; another sold everything needed for the home.

It was warmer, too. Although the branches of the trees were bare, snow was only visible on the distant hills.

All around them, people were talking and laughing as though they had not a care in the world. They all looked well-fed and healthy. On the other side of the island, families struggled to survive during the Time of Snows and even now some might die before the coming of the Time of New Birth.

While Carrik talked to the small, round man, a group of young people approached Esram. They were playing a game with a ball and a stick and were getting in everyone's way, but no-one rebuked them. When they saw Esram, the young people stopped and stared curiously.

A small, wiry boy with jet black hair spoke to him.

"You cannot belong to this town, for we have not seen you before. I am Jay. What are you called?"

Esram liked him at once, just as he had the small, round sort of man who was talking to Carrik.

"I'm Esram. We have come from the other side of the island, where we still serve the King."

Jay exchanged glances with a girl standing behind him, a girl of about twelve years old, with straight, mouse-coloured hair, a snub nose and small, hazel eyes. Esram noticed that the maidens here did not plait their hair as they did at home, but let it hang loose down their backs.

"Have you ever met the King?" Jay wanted to know.

It was the question Esram had feared and he decided that the only thing to do was to tell the truth.

"I never have," he told them honestly. There was no point in making up a story or repeating what others had told him.

The girl sighed impatiently. "You see, Jay? He cannot help us! We need to find someone who knows more!"

"Help you do what?" Esram wanted to know. He thought the girl was rude.

Jay glared at her. "Be quiet, Holly! We do not know yet what he has to say... Let us go back to the game." He turned to Esram. "Shall you join in?"

Esram shook his head. "I should stay with my uncle until I find out what we are to do. Maybe we shall have another time?"

"Maybe. Bye, Esram!"

The young people ran off, laughing and shouting, and Esram returned to Carrik, who was still in earnest conversation with the small, round man and did not even notice him.

Then, ignoring Esram, Carrik followed this man towards the town square. Esram, annoyed, walked along behind.

Once there, Carrik passed his bundle of belongings to Esram and climbed up to a platform in the centre of the square.

As he stood there, looking and feeling sadly out of place, a crowd of people gathered round to see the strangers. Esram's heart began to thump loudly. What if the people did not like what they had come to say? They might attack them with sticks, or throw stones at them.

"What do you have to sell?" a woman shouted, and the silence was broken.

Carrik started to speak. "I do not sell to you. What I have to give is free! Good people, we are strangers here and you are making us welcome. For that, we thank you! I am Carrik and this is my nephew, Esram. We have come all the way from the other side of Karensa, from a land still ruled by the King. It was the King who sent us here."

"How can the King have sent you?" a man wanted to know. "Folk are no longer allowed to go to the Royal Palace!"

"Aye, that is so!" another cried. "Once we could go each evening for the King's help and justice.

Now the King will not let us anywhere near!"

There was a chorus of agreement. Carrik held up his hand for silence.

"All this is true, my friends!" he shouted. "When Lord Bellum disobeyed the King and was cast out of the Palace, war broke out between his followers and the King's people. The King's word decrees that the punishment for disobedience is death, and the King will always honour his word. Because men disobeyed, men should die."

"Then why should we listen to the King?" the first woman wanted to know. "It seems he only wants our death!"

"No, no, that is not so!" Carrik cried. "The King loves each one of you. No! No! This is good news we bring!"

"It sounds it!" a man shouted. Laughter broke out in the crowd.

"It is good news!" Carrik insisted. "The King loved us so much that he sent his own son, Salvis, to die in our place!"

"I heard that," the same woman said. "Lord Bellum killed Salvis... Salvis is dead!"

That cry was taken up by many. Esram saw Carrik lift his hands up and he seemed to be speaking to someone. Esram knew that his uncle was crying to Salvis to help him, and that Salvis would hear him from the Royal Palace without Carrik even speaking out loud, and he knew that help was already on its way.

"No, he is not! He is not dead! Bellum did kill him, I was there! But Salvis lives again and will plead for anyone who turns back to the King. He has taken our punishment for us so that we can once again speak to the King! We do not have to go to the Royal Palace any more! If we trust in Lord Salvis, the King will hear us, right where we are!"

He paused briefly, and when he spoke again, his voice was quite different. He began to speak with authority. "Salvis lives! He overcame death for us! Turn to him now, friends! He loves each one of you! He loves you so much! You cannot understand how much he cares about his people until you turn to him yourself! He will forgive you! He forgave me, even me, with all the wicked things I had done! There is no-one like him in the whole world, nor will there ever be one like him again! Let him fill your heart with his love and his peace! Receive his mighty power! Become the King's people once more!"

He stopped, and there was a deep silence, broken as someone began to sob. As Esram remembered the night he had asked Salvis to forgive him, he, too, was moved.

When Carrik spoke of the love that was in the King's own heart, Salvis drew so close to them that it seemed they could almost touch him. Surely, even the hardest heart must melt at these words?

Esram was so proud of his uncle, but he knew that from this moment, Carrik belonged to the King, that Carrik's own needs and the needs of his family and friends would now take second place to his love for the King. Carrik had been forgiven more than any of them. Now he had a burning in his heart to serve Salvis that none could equal, and not even death would put out this flame.

Then, from the back of the crowd, came the voice of Tomas, leader of the Guardians.

"We do not need the King! We have no king nor lord, neither do we desire any!"

"That's right," someone agreed. "The King brings trouble, not peace. The Guardians take good care of us! We have all we need and we do not quarrel or fight. We already live in peace. Why should we put ourselves under the King's law again? We do not need this!"

The weeping stopped and once more there was silence, broken again by Tomas.

"My dear friends," he said kindly to Carrik and Esram, "We understand that you mean well but we really do not need this King, and we do not need his son Salvis, either. You are deceived. When a man dies, he is dead. He cannot come back and live again... Now, why not find a place to stay this night and then return to your own country in the morning... That is, if your King will allow it!"

Laughter broke out again and one by one people began to leave. They smiled kindly at Carrik and patted Esram on the head, which he hated.

Carrik sat down on the edge of the platform and covered his face with his hands. Tomas had destroyed the moment.

When all the others had gone, the small, round man was left on his own. He held out his hand to Carrik and he was not laughing as the others had laughed.

"As I have told you already, I am Reuben, a boot-maker. I would like to hear more of what you have to say, friend Carrik. Would you and the boy do me the honour of staying at my house? I have plenty of room."

Carrik looked up and took his hand. "Reuben,

we will. The honour is ours."

He took his belongings from Esram, and as he did so he whispered, "Nephew, I feel this is our man of peace."

Esram whispered back, "Uncle, you said yourself it is not going to be easy. Do not lose heart because they laughed."

"I have not," said Carrik, "and neither must you. We are both going to be tested in this place."

Chapter 4

Lord Bellum's power

On the other side of the island, beyond the high moors and across the Meadow of Flowers, the stronghold castle of Lord Bellum stood black and stark against the snow of the Dark Forest, forbidding even in today's pale sunlight.

The stronghold was surrounded by an eerie silence, for here no creature stirred or bird sang. Within these walls no animal dared venture and no bird would fly, except for the vulture and the raven.

Tomas and his daughter, Lindis, were shown into the main hall of the castle, where a huge fire of logs and sweet fir cones blazed in the hearth. This vast hall was decorated with rich tapestries and gold leaf, but for all its splendour, the silks woven into the tapestries were dull and the golden ornaments had no shine.

In the centre of the hall stood a dais on which was placed a great, throne-like chair of carved wood. Above this was a canopy of black velvet with fringes and tassles of gold, and on this elevated throne sat Lord Bellum.

Magnificent as ever, he leant forward in his seat, his jewelled hands tapping impatiently. No crown adorned his black hair, but the chain of gold and precious gems around his neck set him apart as someone of great importance, as did the priceless green emerald hanging from his ear. His tunic was of dark green velvet and his golden cloak was lined with green silk and trimmed with fur. And his face was as handsome as ever.

Lindis made sure she stayed behind her father as they edged nervously across the hall. She was scared. She had heard terrible things about Lord Bellum and had not wanted to come here with Tomas, but he had insisted. He said Lord Bellum had especially asked to meet her. Lindis could not think why this should be, for she had never seen Bellum before. Now, as she looked on him for the first time, she was attracted by his splendour, in spite of her fear.

"It is enough I have summoned you. Do I now have to wait for you to come?" Lord Bellum's voice was deep and musical.

They hurried to the platform and as Tomas fell on his face before the throne, Lindis copied him. Bellum expected worship from those who desired to serve him.

"You are Tomas, leader of the Guardians of the far side of the island?" Bellum asked.

Tomas tried to preserve his dignity, but in his present position this was impossible.

"I am Tomas, lord," he agreed.

"This is your daughter? No – no, let the child answer for herself."

"Yes, sir," she murmured, obviously very afraid.

Bellum's manner changed. His voice became soft. When it pleased him, he could be so charming, but it was a deceit, a lie. Always Bellum would deceive. It was in his very nature to tell lies.

"Come, child, stand up," he said gently. Then, not so gently, "No, not you, Tomas. I would speak to your daughter first. Child, come here, come close to me."

Trembling, Lindis obeyed, and as she stood before him, Bellum took note of her thick, dark brown hair, her large brown eyes and smooth olive skin.

He placed a long, slender finger beneath her chin and tilted her face upwards.

"You are a nut-brown maid," he smiled. "What is your name?"

"Lindis, sir."

"How old are you, Lindis?"

"Thirteen, sir."

"Lord," Bellum corrected her, still in the same soft voice. "You must always call me 'lord', for that is what I am."

"Yes, sir... lord."

"That is better. Well, Lindis, you find favour with me. I believe you may be of value to me as I build my empire."

Lindis tried not to shudder. She did not want to be of value to Bellum, or to anyone else really. Lindis liked the good things of life. She liked her father being leader of the town where she lived. She liked her comfortable home where her mother and father doted on her. She wished she was there now, but only in part; part of Lindis was enjoying this.

"How can I help you, lord? I am no-one. Only a child."

"Ah yes, but the young serve me best, if they are willing. Are you willing, Lindis?"

Lindis hung her head and did not reply. Suddenly

she had a bad feeling, deep in the pit of her stomach, a feeling of dread and foreboding.

Tomas, now getting uncomfortable on the floor, cleared his throat and coughed to attract attention.

Bellum pretended to be surprised. "Tomas, my friend, I had forgotten you. Get up, man. Come here and stand with your daughter."

Thankfully, Tomas did as he was told.

"So... father and daughter... You shall serve me well. Listen to what I have to say. Yesterday you received visitors to the town? A man and a boy?"

"Yes, lord. Harmless fools, we thought, trying to persuade the people to give up the society we have built and return to the King."

At the mention of the King, Bellum's face darkened with anger, his eyes amber in the light from the fire.

"Harmless fools?" he roared. Tomas and Lindis began to quake. "These are not harmless fools! Carrik was once my highest servant and Esram defied me by stealing away a maiden about to be put to death! Oh no, Tomas, these are not harmless! They are dangerous, to you and to me."

"What... what can we do, then, lord?" Tomas stammered.

Bellum's mood changed again. He became calm once more, but this time he spoke decisively.

"This, Tomas, is what you must do. The people in the town do not want the King in their lives because they have every comfort. You must see that this continues. Take care of their every need. If you need money to do this, come to me. They must want for nothing, do you understand? They will never even think of obeying the King, or Salvis either. In return, Tomas," he leant forward towards them, "you shall have all the wealth and power you desire. What do you say? Will you serve me?"

Tomas did not hesitate. At the mention of power, his eyes narrowed with greed. More than wealth, more than jewels, more than land, Tomas desired power.

"Yes, lord, I will serve you," he replied.

Bellum nodded. "Now, Lindis, what of you? Your task will be to see that the children never hear the story Carrik is telling, and if they do hear, then they must not believe it. Your reward will be wealth to equal that of your father, and when you are older, the husband of your choice."

"She will obey you, lord," Tomas said quickly. "She is a good maiden. I have never yet had to beat her, but if needs be, I will do so now. I will see that she obeys."

Lindis gasped. She could not believe her own father, who had never raised his hand to her, was saying these things!

Bellum paused, then he nodded. "First, you must swear to serve me only and forsake the King for ever. Are you so willing?"

Tomas agreed. "I am ready, lord."

"Kneel before me," Bellum commanded and when Tomas did so, he stretched out his hand towards him.

"Tomas, you forsake anything that is of the King, you pledge to serve only me. I accept you as my servant."

Tomas looked up. His face appeared changed. Lindis was almost afraid of him.

"Now the child," Bellum ordered.

Lindis took an involuntary step backwards, but Tomas stood up right behind her. Bellum was in front of her. She could not escape. Part of Lindis did not want to escape. She was curious. At the same time, she was sickened by Lord Bellum. Part of her wanted to turn and run as fast as she could, back home to her mother's side.

"Lindis, stand straight and hold out your hands," Bellum told her. "Towards me, that is right." His voice grew stronger. "Lindis, are you also willing?"

Lindis' curiosity defeated her revulsion.

"I am willing, lord," she said, but her voice was husky with fear.

She swayed as waves of darkness fell over her and slowly, a dreadful power surged through her, its icy fingers gripping her heart, forcing away all love and compassion.

When she looked up, she was no longer afraid. She laughed aloud, a harsh, cruel laugh, and Bellum laughed with her.

"Ah, my daughter, now you will do as I ask?"

"Master, I will do anything you ask. Anything."

Yet even as they left the hall and walked out into the pale sunlight, Lindis regretted what she had done but knew that it was too late to change her mind.

The laughter, which was not real laughter at all, died on her lips, and in its place were a thousand tears to mourn the love she had so easily thrown away.

But she was unable to shed the tears, because her heart had become as cold and hard as stone.

Chapter 5

Holly

Esram stretched and pulled the bedcovers up around his shoulders. He was too comfortable and too warm to get up yet. Sleeping in a room of his own, in a real bed with a feather mattress, was a wonderful luxury after his straw pallet in Petroc's farmhouse.

On this side of the island, life was much easier. Food was plentiful and good. Carrik and Esram had not eaten so well for a long time, not since they had left Lord Bellum's castle. After spending yesterday recovering from their long journey, they were ready to begin the work that the King had given them to do.

Not yet though. For now, Esram wanted to stay beneath the warm bed covers and think of what had happened in the last two days.

In spite of the discomforts of life on the other side of Karensa, Esram missed Petroc and his sister, Morwen. He had never met anyone as fearless as Petroc, and Esram desperately wanted to be brave himself, yet so many times he was afraid. Morwen had told him once that he was every bit as brave as Petroc because he had risked his own life to rescue her from Lord Bellum's castle, but Esram didn't think he was brave. He had been terrified. Morwen just hadn't realised the fear he had felt inside.

Esram missed Morwen more than anyone else. She was very special to him. Her fierce loyalty to the King was gradually being revealed in her gentle manner, in her quiet boldness and her caring heart. Esram wanted to be like Morwen, too. But Petroc and Morwen were not here, and he and Carrik had been given work to do.

He sighed deeply and got up at last, crossing over to the small window beneath the eaves.

Reuben's house was large and rambling and not quite straight. From the street below, the tall, narrow building appeared to lean to one side. On the ground floor at the front of the house was the shop where Reuben made and mended boots, cutting and trimming, gluing, stitching and hammering over his wooden lasts. Esram liked this shop. Boots to be repaired were hanging up on one side and on the other, boots ready for collection. In the window was a selection of new boots for sale. The shop had a special smell of new leather and glue.

Behind the shop was a large, cosy kitchen warmed by a huge range, over which hung an assortment of copper pots and pans. As well as a wooden table and chairs, there was a comfortable settle by the fire.

Reuben and Holly had a room each on the next floor, and now so did Carrik. Esram's room was at the very top of the house, where there were other rooms that were not used.

The house was so comfortable, but Esram's heart was at the simple farm with the friends who had shown him the first real kindness he had ever known.

From the window, he looked down across the roof-tops to the sea, to a harbour where many fishing boats bobbed up and down with the tide. Already fishermen were seated on the harbour walls mending their nets. The sun was sparkling on the light ground frost which would soon disappear.

This was a beautiful land, a land of plenty. Only one thing was missing, but that was the most important thing of all.

Esram heard breakfast being prepared so he splashed his face with cold water from the bowl on the dresser, hurriedly threw on his tunic and trousers, pulled on his boots and went downstairs.

Reuben handed him a plate of hot, golden-brown sausages.

"Here you are, boy, some nourishment you need. Turn you sideways on and we should lose you!" he exclaimed.

Esram looked at Reuben's rounded form and was not sure he wanted to look like him. However, he was hungry, so he cleared his plate, and he ate the crusty bread and jam that followed and drank a beaker of warm goat's milk, too.

Carrik and Reuben were doing quite a lot of talking. In fact, they were doing so much talking that Esram had not seen much of his uncle since they had arrived. Carrik had only one thing on his mind; how to start the work of winning the people of the town back to the King.

This meant that Esram was left with Holly, Reuben's daughter. Esram was not sure about Holly, either. As he helped her clear away the plates, he thought of Morwen again. Today, Holly wore a tunic of rich, red wool decorated with shiny beads, and her hair was tied back with a red ribbon, but her hair was still straight and mouse-coloured and her hazel eyes were still small and she was uninteresting compared to the lovely Morwen.

Esram reminded himself that a person's heart was important, not their looks, and besides, he was here to do the King's work, so when Holly told him that today she would show him the town, he didn't argue. It was unwise to argue with Holly. She was used to getting her own way. Holly told folk what to do; she did not ask.

Holly and Esram walked down to the harbour where, one by one, the boats were leaving for the day's fishing. They climbed on to the harbour wall and sat in the sun. It had only been a day's journey to the far side of Karensa, yet it was so warm here that it seemed like a different world. All that was needed to keep warm was a thin cloak over their tunics.

"Is it still the Time of Snows?" Esram asked, wondering if somehow the seasons were different in this part of the island.

"We do not see much snow here," Holly explained.

"Where I come from, there's lots of snow. It snows for months, and it's very cold."

Holly pulled a face. "I should not like that. You will do better here."

Again, Esram was not so sure. He looked behind them to where the white-walled houses of the town gave way to open green countryside. This truly was a beautiful land, seemingly free from trouble or hardship.

"Tell me about your home," Holly prompted. It was a demand, not a request.

Esram suppressed a sigh. He didn't really want to tell Holly too much about his past, for he hardly knew her, but her father had been kind to them. Something told him that if he wanted to win people over to the King, he must first get to know them. This had to begin with trust.

"I don't have a home," he began. "Not of my own. I don't know what became of my parents but my Uncle Carrik brought me up in his own household, until we all went to live with Lord Bellum in his castle. It was in my uncle's house that I met Petroc, then he came to the castle with us."

"Petroc? Who is he?"

"He was my uncle's prisoner. Uncle Carrik and Lord Bellum and... and I... were... were not kind to Petroc."

"Why?" She stared at him and he felt his face turn red, but he was going to tell the truth, even though it hurt. It was what the King expected of those who served him.

"Because," he explained, "we served Bellum then, and Petroc was, and always will be, loyal to the King. Holly, Petroc is the bravest person I know."

"Where is he now?"

"When Bellum killed Lord Salvis, the King's son, all Bellum's prisoners had to be set free. Petroc is now back on his farm."

"When did you and your uncle leave the castle?"

"Ah well, that's another tale. Petroc has a sister

called Morwen and Morwen made me realise that the best thing to do was to serve the King, so I did. Next day, Carrik did, too." Esram decided that maybe he was telling Holly too much. "That's enough about me. Now it's your turn, Holly. Tell me about your life. Where has your mother gone?"

To his dismay, Holly's face changed. Her lip trembled and she wouldn't look at him, staring instead across the sea.

"My mother died last year. She was sick."

Esram's smile froze. So they did have trouble here after all, for here was sickness they could not cure.

"I'm sorry, Holly," he murmured, not knowing what else to say. He should have known that her mother would not have left her unless there was a good reason.

"It's not your fault, is it?" She jutted her chin out defiantly. It was a gesture Esram was to come to know well. "We cannot bring her back by shedding more tears, can we? I feel sorry for you, really. At least I had my mother with me for twelve years. You never knew yours, nor your father... Now, I shall show you our town, and I would have you tell me more about Salvis, and the King."

"Really?" Esram was surprised.

"Yes. I said so, did I not? No – no, wait, my friends are coming! Jay and Lindis will want to hear, too."

The black-haired boy who had spoken to Esram on the day they arrived ran towards them. With him was a girl of about thirteen, and as Holly was plain faced, so this girl was pretty, with thick brown hair that fell in soft waves about her small, olive-skinned face and big, dark eyes that sparkled.

"This is Lindis," Holly explained. "Her father is Tomas, the leader of the Guardians. Jay lives on a farm not far from the town." She turned to her friends. "Jay, Lindis, I know you want to hear about Salvis too?"

"Yes, I do," Jay agreed readily, but Lindis interrupted him.

"No, I do not! I want to watch the Guardians on parade in the Town Square, then I want to walk up to the moors to watch the eagles!"

Holly hesitated, then she remembered who Lindis was and decided that it was unwise to upset her.

"Yes, that is what we shall do, then. We can hear about Salvis any time."

Esram bit his lip in disappointment, but at the same time he remembered how unsure he was of what to say and he was also relieved that for the moment, the task had been taken from him.

Chapter 6

The Children of the Second Morning

They stayed on the high moor until the sun began to drift into the mist which surrounded Karensa.

Esram found the moors exciting: the heather-clad hills crowned by rocks of granite where the eagle and the kite soared freely against the clear, grey sky. The high moors were lonely, but they gave him a sense of the King's presence. It reminded him that although the Royal Palace was out of sight, the King cared for this part of Karensa as much as for the land on the other side of the moors.

The young people sat in silence on an outcrop of rock where they had climbed, each of them suddenly aware of power higher and mightier than themselves.

Esram felt at ease with Jay, and also with Holly, but there was something about Lindis he did not like; something that caused his spirit to draw back from her.

Neither did he like the way that Jay and Holly kept whispering together when they thought he was not looking. He was a stranger here and it made him nervous. He watched a great eagle soaring over the hills, trusting in a current of air to keep him airborne. Esram knew he should be like that eagle. He should trust Salvis like that, but Esram was still flapping his wings and trying to do things in his own strength, not using the King's power at all.

As the shadows grew longer, Jay and Lindis left for home.

"We should go too," Esram said to Holly.

"No need. It is not far to the town. Tomorrow it might rain, or be foggy. We should make the most of the day."

Sensing that it was useless to argue with her, Esram let her have her way and they sat there for another half hour. Then, when the light had almost gone, Holly suddenly sprang down from the rock and brushed her clothes.

"We had better go. Father will be concerned."

She ran off ahead. Esram tried to keep up with her but he was unsure of the ground and soon she was out of sight.

"Holly! Holly, come back!" he called.

There was no reply.

"Holly! I don't know the way back to the town!"

There was still no reply.

Esram sighed crossly. He had no idea which way to go now that it was getting dark. He hoped he had chosen the right path.

He stumbled on. Suddenly a heavy weight on his back drove the air from his lungs and sent him crashing to the ground. He struggled as a hood was thrown over his head and his hands were tied behind his back. Too short of breath and too full of fear to speak, he was hauled to his feet and led away across the moor.

It seemed a lifetime before he felt himself pushed through a door and into a chair. The journey had been a nightmare. His captors had moved quickly and Esram, forced to keep up, had fallen over many times and was pulled roughly to his feet. No-one spoke. The silence made him even more afraid. He was worried he might be sick.

He sat on the chair, frightened, dazed and bruised, and trying to recover his breath.

"Who... who are you?" he managed to gasp at last. Still the silence. It made the hairs on the back of his neck prickle. He was sweating, even though the night was becoming cold.

He tried again. "I don't have any money. Nor does my Uncle Carrik. We are poor people. We... we do not even have our own home any more!"

"Be silent!" cried a voice that seemed familiar. "We shall talk. You must listen! We believe you can tell us about this Lord Salvis and about the King?"

"Yes... yes, I can." It was the last thing Esram had expected to hear.

"Are you loyal to this King?"

"I am now." This time there was no hesitation.

Again the silence, broken by muffled whispers. Esram had cramp in his arms and he wished he could see who his captors were. Not seeing them made him feel even more helpless than he was. Then, as he searched for something to say, the hood was pulled from his head.

In the sudden light, Esram blinked and looked straight into the faces of Jay and Holly. They were surrounded by other children of assorted ages and sizes. Esram had been taken prisoner by a group of children!

Jay made a sign to the two bigger boys, the ones

who had captured Esram. "He cannot escape. There are too many of us. Untie his hands."

"Why have you done this to me?" Esram asked in bewilderment as he tried to rub the life back into his arms. "Is it a game, or something?"

"Oh no," Holly said in a quiet voice, "it is no game."

He looked around. He was in a stone barn, furnished sparsely with a few old chairs and a wooden table, and lit by many candles. The candles flickered softly, mellowing the faces of the ten or twelve young people watching him: children of all ages and sizes, children with healthy, well-fed faces and sad eyes.

"No," Esram breathed, suddenly aware of the importance of the task he and Carrik had been given to do. He saw the children as Morwen had once seen him: children with everything, who had nothing. "No, this is not a game. But why did you bring me here in that way?"

Holly sat at his feet. "We had to," she explained. "This is our secret place. We cannot tell you where it is unless you become one of us. If you do not want to help us, we shall put the hood back on and take you back to the town, and no more shall be said."

"But you will join us," said Jay softly. "I know it."

"Who are you? What is it I should join?"

Jay started to speak then changed his mind and gestured to Holly. She took hold of Esram's hand. It was almost as if her bossy self had been left behind on the moors.

"Esram, we are the children of the town. Our parents say they do not want anything to do with

Lord Salvis, or his father the King, but... but we do not agree. We know there are other things we need besides food and warm homes. We know we have an empty place in here," she placed her hand on her heart. "We know the empty place needs to be filled and... and we have searched and searched... and we have not found anything at all..." her voice faded to a whisper.

"The Guardians were formed when the King's Palace became closed to us," Jay went on. "Our parents said it was the dawn of a new morning for the town, but we are waiting for the second morning, when we find what is missing from our hearts. We are called the Children of the Second Morning. Will you help us, Esram?"

"Oh yes," said Esram. "I will help you, Jay, for that is why I am here."

They sat around him in a group, the candlelight softening their young, eager faces and for the first time Esram realised the burden the King had put upon him. Then, just as he was ready to speak, it was as though a voice whispered in his ear, "You do not know enough to tell others, do you?"

And Esram listened to the voice instead of trusting the King.

"I will tell you some," he hesitated. "But I do not know all there is to tell."

"Anything," said Jay. "Anything, Esram. What we see in you, we want too. There is something different about you. Something we do not understand."

Esram looked down at them. The youngest girl could only have been five or six years old, yet she knew that there was something missing in her life. She listened as well as the others as Esram told them the story of how Bellum, a lord of the King's Palace, led many people to disobey the King, and of how the King loved his people so much that he had sent his son, Salvis, to die in their place. For that, Salvis now lived again, for ever.

"Tell us about Salvis," Holly whispered. "What does he look like? What sort of person is he?"

Esram hung his head and could not look into their eager faces.

"He is a wonderful person, but... but... I never met him face to face. The first time I saw him was in Lord Bellum's castle on the night he died. The second time was from far away."

"Then how can you talk about him as you do?" Holly cried.

"Because I have pledged my loyalty to him. When I did that, it was as though I had known him all my life. He forgave me all the things I had done to hurt him and he filled that empty place inside my heart... He will do that for you now, if you desire it."

He held his breath. Just as when Carrik had spoken to the people in the town square, there was silence. One little girl was crying. Then a voice was raised in protest. Lindis did not agree.

"Do not listen to him! My father has made a comfortable life for you! Surely you cannot want to return to the King with all his rules? 'Do not do this, do not do that!'"

"It is not like that!" Esram protested, wondering what Lindis was doing here.

"It is exactly like that!" Lindis retorted.

It seemed as though a quarrel would break out but Jay put a stop to it, holding up his hand for silence.

"We must consider what Esram has said. Will you come and talk to us again? Will you be part of the Children of the Second Morning?"

Even though he was disappointed that no-one had wanted to turn to the King, Esram agreed.

"Swear never to reveal our secret place and swear never to tell anyone about us," Jay commanded.

"I shall watch you, Esram," Holly added, once more her bossy self. "I shall know if you tell a soul!"

"You do not need to watch me," Esram told her in a quiet, serious voice. "I shall not tell a single person, I swear. I know you will find that which you seek."

Outwardly calm, he did the thing he should have done before he started to speak, he called silently to Salvis, knowing that the King's son would not fail him.

Salvis... Lord Salvis... If you want me to do this for you, send me the help I need!

"We had better go now. It is past supper time," Holly said, then to Jay, "Do we trust him?"

Jay nodded. "I trust him. This is my father's barn so if Esram betrays us, I shall be the first one to be punished."

"I shall not betray you."

As they left, Jay named the children, one by one. A new hope stirred in Esram's heart. He just knew that something exciting was going to happen in Jay's barn.

Chapter 7

The call of Karensa

The King's Palace stood at the centre of the island of Karensa and the Great Hall stood in the centre of the Palace, for this was Karensa's heart. From here came power and authority, hope, justice and love.

At the far end of the Hall stood three thrones before which the King's servants sang praises day and night.

On the middle throne sat the King, splendid in golden robes, the jewels in his crown reflected in the marble floor below. The King's presence was unchanging and timeless and although he had grey hair and beard, his face was neither young nor old and shone with a silver light which gave light to all around.

On his right sat his only son, the Lord Salvis, no longer a peasant but now as awesome as the King. Salvis had been given robes of shining white. Fire shone in his eyes but so did great love. His crown sent rays of light flashing in every direction so that his head was surrounded by a moving aura. His face was brighter than the sun, and as the King's face shone like silver, so Salvis' face shone like pure gold.

The third throne was the seat of the Unseen Lord and from here glowed a light the colour of a rose sunset.

The three thrones, although separate, were also One, and the King's servants worshipped all three Lords as One, as they always had and always would for all of eternity.

Salvis turned to his father, the King.

"Lord and Father, you promised once that I should never lose even one of my followers?"

"That was my word."

"Then, Lord King, mighty Father, you should know that someone dear to my heart is moving away from me."

The King inclined his head. "This I already know. My servant, Veritan, told me of it, but it is not Veritan's place to plead for people, only to obey. You are the one chosen to plead, because you are the one who died. You speak of Luke, who once stayed on Karensa?"

"Yes, Father. Luke was loyal to me, almost to the very end, but now he is making other things more important than me."

"Yes, I know, my son. Once my word is given I will abide by it. In that way, my word will still be as true at the end of time as it was at the beginning."

"So you will send help, Father?"

"I will do more than that. You heard Esram's cry from the far side of the island? We shall answer that, too. They both have a destiny to serve us. We will draw Luke back, and together, their pleas will be answered. Are we agreed?"

Salvis smiled. When Salvis smiled it was as though Karensa smiled with him.

"Yes, mighty Father, we are agreed."

The King and the Son raised their hands, palms outwards, towards the Unseen Lord.

The rose-coloured light deepened to blood red, and then it moved around the Great Hall, and the lights of silver and gold made way for its passage. Three times it moved around the Great Hall and as it passed over the King's servants, their praises grew louder and louder, the notes of their anthems higher and more beautiful each time; songs with words of ancient days which only those who occupied the Three Thrones knew the meaning of.

The light faded and settled and returned to the colour of a gentle sunset.

In its movement, power had gone from the Three Thrones. The Unseen Lord was ready to make war against the Prince of the world. His destination was the Cornish fishing village of Poldawn.

Luke could not wait to get out of church and Rosie had to run to catch up with him as he strode down the narrow path to the gate, slipping and sliding in the snow which had now started to thaw. Once outside the church gate, he stopped and allowed Rosie to catch up.

"What's the matter with you?" she panted. "If you hate church so much, why go?"

"I don't hate it," he muttered, digging his hands deeper into the pockets of his fleece.

"You've been in a bad mood since Christmas Eve, and that was a week ago," Rosie grumbled. "What's upset you?"

"Nothing," he growled.

"It doesn't seem like it!" she snapped, trying to keep up with him. "I thought... We've been happy, lately, all of us. Or I thought we had, since we... since we left the island..."

"I saw him!" Luke muttered.

"Who? You saw who?"

"Him! I saw... *him*... in the park, on Christmas Eve."

Rosie pulled her hood over her long, fair curls.

"Luke," she sighed. "Who did you see on Christmas Eve?" She giggled. "Don't tell me you saw Santa Claus?"

Luke's steely grey eyes glared at her but they had no effect, because she was no longer scared of him. Luke had changed since they both stayed on the island. He hardly ever lost his temper. Besides, now that Rosie was ten, she knew better than to be scared of her own brother.

"Of course not!" he snarled. Then, still glaring at her, he added, "It was Salvis!"

Rosie ran in front of him so that he was forced to stop.

"How could you have seen Salvis? Salvis lives on Karensa!"

"He was here in Poldawn on Christmas Eve, in the park."

Suddenly, Luke was not glaring any more, and Rosie knew that he was telling the truth.

"What did he say?" she whispered.

Luke shook his head. He couldn't bring himself to share it with her.

"I can't remember," he lied.

"Yes you can! And why didn't I see him? Why didn't he speak to me? I miss him too! I – oh no!"

"What?"

"I've left my Bible in church. We shall have to go back for it. Dad will go manic if I lose anything else."

"You go. I'll wait here."

Rosie looked over her shoulder. It was nearly dark and the trees in the lane made strange shapes against the night sky.

"No, you come," she pleaded. "Look, we don't have to go through the front gate. We can take a short cut and go in the back way."

Luke sighed. "OK, I s'pose we must! But I wish you didn't forget things, Rosie! Come on."

They retraced their steps, then turned to the left and followed the stone wall.

Suddenly, Luke stopped. "Hang on a minute, Rosie! I never saw this door before."

"Neither did I."

Puzzled, they examined the door. It was made of thick oak and had bolts of black iron and a heavy iron ring for a handle. Rosie turned the handle and pushed the door but it wouldn't move.

"That's funny," she said. "It's not locked, yet I can't move it."

Luke nudged her out of the way. "Here, let me try."

He turned the ring. It moved easily. He pushed the door. It creaked open.

"Find the door only you can unlock..."

The words Salvis had spoken to him returned to him now and with them: *"I will never leave you or forsake you."*

They looked through the open door. The church was gone. In its place they saw a land of green pastures and orchards, and beyond this land, the sea.

"Karensa," Luke breathed. "Rosie, it's the island! I know it! Look at the sea! The mist is there on the horizon, just as it always was!"

"It looks different," Rosie said, hesitating. "Where is the Dark Forest? The Dark Forest used to be everywhere!"

"It must be a different part of the island, a part we don't know." He moved to go through the door, but Rosie held back.

"Luke, think! If we go through there we may not be able to get back! At least not for ages. Remember last time. We were there for nearly a year. Think of the dangers, Luke! Think of the straw mattresses! Think of the boring food and no telly, and work instead of school... and people... people get killed on Karensa. Think about Bellum!"

Luke closed his eyes, trying to make sense of his thoughts. Karensa was calling him. Salvis was calling him. It was like going home. The call on his life was strong and he couldn't deny it.

He felt Salvis close to them, so very close, so close that he could almost feel his great heart beating. Just to be there, on Karensa again... The call grew stronger and stronger.

He walked through the door, and, just as she had done when she had climbed into the boat with him the first time, Rosie went with him now, slipping her hand trustingly into his.

The door swung shut behind them, and when they looked back, the door and the stone wall had gone. They were alone in a land they knew and yet did not know. As they stood hand in hand, Poldawn faded away to a memory and Karensa became reality.

Chapter 8

Unfamiliar ground

They were in a narrow, twisting lane with high hedges, branches bare and brown against a cold grey sky. Behind them the open moors were purple with heather and crowned with granite rocks, the very highest capped with snow. Below them was a small town, surrounded on three sides by sea. Although the day was clear and cold, the horizon was obscured by mist.

"Is it really the island, Luke?" Rosie asked, frowning. "It doesn't look like the island, does it? And if it's still winter, where has all the snow gone? There was much more snow than this on Karensa. Where is it?"

Luke sighed. "Why d'you think I know all the answers to everything, Rosie?"

"Because you tell everybody you do."

"Well, this really is Karensa. I can feel it. Inside. In here." He put his hand on his heart. "This must be a part of Karensa we didn't go to before. People did talk about the far side of the island. This must be it."

"But... but... we won't know anyone, will we? I want to see Petroc and Morwen. And Martha. I want to see Martha... I did love Martha. She was like another mum to us."

"We didn't know anyone last time, did we? Not

at first. I... I suppose we could go to the King. That's what we did before, and he sorted things out."

"Where? Where to the King? Where's the Royal Palace? Where's the Dark Forest? Oh, I don't like it here! I wish I'd never come! I really wish I'd never come!"

"No you don't. You're such a baby, Rosie. You were just as brave as anyone else in the past, so be brave now."

Rosie's lip trembled. She did try to be brave. The King had told her once that she would learn to be brave, but that all seemed a long time ago, and she didn't feel very brave at the moment. She wanted to go home. There would be a fire in the hearth and the TV switched on and supper nearly ready. Rosie was hungry. At home they still had loads of food to eat up after Christmas. She could just manage a sausage roll, or a few mince pies.

Luke ran his fingers through his fair hair. The truth was, he didn't know what to do, but he wasn't going to admit it.

As they stood thinking, they both felt a sort of calm, as though peace was all around them.

"Salvis is here!" Luke said triumphantly. "That's why we've come! To find Salvis again! I know what we must do. We must go where there are people. Come on, Rosie, let's go down the lane towards that town!"

Once again, Rosie followed him.

By the time they reached the town, evening shadows were lengthening and it was getting cold.

"This is weird," Luke muttered. "It's Karensa,

53

yet it's not! There were never shops on Karensa before! And everything seems so clean!"

The streets were almost deserted because people had gone home for supper, but one small group remained outside a crooked little shop that sold boots.

Luke and Rosie thought it best to watch these people from the safety of the street corner until they found out how friendly they were. There were dangers on Karensa they did not face at home and it was wise to be cautious.

"Let's go and ask them where we are," Rosie suggested.

"Rosie, don't be stupid! We can't just go up to them and say, 'Where are we?' What would they think of us? How would we explain how we got here?"

Rosie didn't reply. She was close to tears, and Luke was a little bit sorry for what he had said. Feelings seemed more important on Karensa than at home.

"We could stand at the back and listen to what they're saying? That way we might find out where we are?"

"I suppose so."

They edged over to the crowd and stood where they would not be noticed, feeling conspicuous in their hoods, fleeces and jeans. Luke was very aware of his short hair. Boys and men on Karensa grew their hair down to their shoulders.

"It is Karensa," Rosie whispered. "See how they're dressed, Luke. I remember now. Everyone wears trousers and tunics and boots. Luke, it *is* Karensa." Quite suddenly she beamed, all her fears forgotten. "We're home, Luke! We've come home!"

Luke felt a lump the size of a tennis ball in his throat, because Karensa really did feel more like home than Poldawn. Now they were actually on the island, it was as if their life in Cornwall was just a dream.

"Why, Rosie? Why does it seem like home? We've never been to this part of Karensa before."

"It's because Salvis is close," she said simply. "We don't have to know how to find the Royal Palace. Salvis is here. The island is his home."

Luke was getting emotional, so, to hide his feelings, he said, "Ssh, listen to what's being said."

Rosie smiled. She knew that her brother felt the same as she did.

Most of the people were listening to one man talk, a man who had long, fairish hair and a beard and whose face was thin and sharp-featured. Luke saw him first and as he recognised this man, his blood froze.

Then Rosie knew him, too.

"Oh no," she breathed. "It's Carrik!"

At the very same moment, Carrik saw them. He recognised them at once. At first he looked pleased to see them, then he saw the horror on their faces and his expression became guarded.

He inclined his head slightly to acknowledge them, but that was all. He continued to talk to the group, and it seemed he was telling them about the King and about his son, Salvis, who had died for them. The crowd didn't seem very interested. They listened politely, but when two soldiers approached, they drifted away. These soldiers were not Bellum's men, who always wore his emblem of a serpent. These soldiers were dressed in dark grey tunics with vests of chain mail, and cloaks of midnight blue. When the crowd walked away, the soldiers went too.

They were left alone with Carrik. Rosie clung to Luke's hand very, very tightly.

Carrik spoke first. "So you have come back to Karensa, Luke and Rosie. I am surprised to see you here. This is not the side of Karensa you would remember."

"I remember you!" Luke blurted out. "You hated us!"

Carrik didn't falter. "Yes, I did," he agreed. "But Luke, things have changed. I have asked the King to forgive me for the wrong things I did and I've placed my life in his hands."

"Huh! People don't change! Not that much, they don't."

"Oh, they do, Luke, they do," Carrik said softly. "The King had much to forgive me, but he was willing, and now I have come here to win this town back to him."

They stared, not knowing what to say.

"Do you have a place to stay?" Carrik asked them.

Luke shook his head. "We've only just arrived."

"I see. Well, I can solve that problem for you at least. Follow me, please."

Feeling helpless and very alone, they obeyed, but neither of them was happy about it. How could they trust this man who had been so cruel to them?

Carrik led them into the boot-maker's shop.

"Wait there," he instructed, and disappeared into a back room. He returned a few minutes later with a small, round sort of man with rosy cheeks, brown hair and blue eyes.

"Children, this is Reuben. He owns this shop and this house. He has said you may stay here with us. Reuben wants to know more about Salvis. He is a friend."

The children exchanged uneasy glances. They didn't want to stay with Carrik's friends. Carrik had been so cruel to Petroc. They might get up tomorrow morning and find that he had made them his prisoners!

Reuben held out his hand, which was hard and calloused from his work as a maker of boots.

"Welcome. I heard of two children who lived with the Lord Salvis in the Bay of Dolphins. Are you those children?"

They nodded silently.

"Then you are twice welcome. Come and meet my daughter."

In the large, comfortable kitchen behind the shop, sat a girl with straight, mouse-coloured hair and a plain face.

"This is Holly."

Holly stared at them and didn't look at all friendly.

"And this," Reuben went on, "is my friend Carrik's nephew, Esram."

A tall, fair-haired youth stood up to meet them. He was a younger version of Carrik.

Luke and Rosie were dismayed. They didn't want to be with these people, who they didn't know. They certainly didn't want to be with Carrik. They wanted to be at the Bay of Dolphins with Petroc and Morwen and with Salvis.

Then Esram said kindly, "Sit down, both of you. You look tired. Many things have happened since you left Karensa, and later when you are rested, I shall tell you of them. For a while, my uncle and myself lived with Petroc and Morwen. They have now rebuilt their father's farm. It was Morwen who helped me when I wanted to give my life to the King. They both miss you, very much. Petroc would always speak kindly of you, Luke, almost as a brother."

With those words, everything changed.

Chapter 9

Bay of Perils

For the next three days it rained, never once stopping long enough for the children to leave the house. The rain washed away the last of the snow from the high moors, and then on the fourth day, the sun came out. Within the hour the cobbled streets were dry.

After breakfast, Holly suggested that all the young people went out for a walk.

"There is a special place I want to show you," she explained. "A place not even Esram has seen yet."

Tired of being kept indoors, they readily agreed, and Rosie helped Holly to clear away the breakfast plates and wash them up. One thing they did not have here was washing-up liquid and washing greasy plates without soap wasn't a pleasant task. Grease stuck to everything, especially to Rosie's hands.

Rosie didn't know what to think of Holly. Luke said he liked her, but then, Luke probably recognised himself in lots of things Holly said and did. She was too bossy for Rosie, who, like Esram, let her have her own way for the sake of a quiet life.

While the girls cleared the dishes, Luke and Esram fetched logs from the back yard. Luke was still wary of Esram and even more wary of Carrik. How could either of them be trusted? How could

Petroc and Morwen possibly have forgiven Carrik for what he did to their family?

"He killed their own father," Luke once whispered to Rosie. "I could never forgive someone who did that, could you?"

Rosie was thoughtful. "Well," she said slowly, "The Bible does say we should forgive."

"Yes, but... *that*?"

"So much is different here now," Rosie replied. "It's hard to take it all in. At least we have proper beds, and our own rooms. On the other side of the island we had to sleep on straw. And at least I don't have to do my hair in those horrible plaits like I did before."

Luke sighed. "Sometimes, Rosie, you are one sad person, did you know that?"

"Why?"

"We were having a serious conversation, then you start talking about plaiting your hair."

"You didn't have to do it," she pointed out. "When Martha did my hair, she plaited so tight I thought my scalp was being pulled off... That reminds me, Reuben wants us to wear 'proper' clothes."

Luke had groaned. "Oh no! Surely our sweatshirts and jeans are OK? They're not that different from the clothes they wear."

However, next morning, he found a dark brown tunic and trousers left out in his bedroom together with a pair of soft, high boots. Rosie appeared later wearing the same sort of clothes, only blue.

They exchanged glances. "Here we go again!" Luke grinned.

"At least they're comfortable," Rosie replied.

"They'll have to be. Our own clothes have been taken away. We really are back on the island now, Luke."

"And who knows when we'll go home?" he replied.

As soon as he could, Esram had told them some of the changes that had taken place since they had gone home to Poldawn.

Salvis now lived in the Royal Palace, but the King had given his own power to each one of his followers. Now it was possible to talk to the King at any time, just in the quiet of their hearts. They did not have to go to the Palace to speak to the King any more. He heard them no matter where they were.

They also had the power to heal people, just like Salvis had done, and to praise the King in special words.

Bellum's castle was even darker now and many more people had deserted the King's service to join him.

Martha and Delfi, her adopted daughter, had spent the Time of Snows here, on her brother's farm, not far from the town. Martha had been ill and the climate was kinder here. She had gone home now that she was better, disliking the Guardians and missing her own family. Delfi had stayed, but she was rarely seen.

Petroc had recovered from the time he had spent as a prisoner in Bellum's castle. He was now fit and healthy again and had put on weight. He was healed in his spirit, too.

Another girl had lived with them, a girl called

Cherry. This girl had met Petroc in Bellum's castle, where she had been taken by her mistress, Zena. Now Zena was widowed and was free to return to her parents' home, because, unlike her husband, she had never pledged her loyalty to Bellum. Cherry had gone with her, back to the place where she had once been so happy.

"How is Morwen?" Luke could not resist asking.

Rosie giggled. She knew her brother liked Morwen very much.

Esram's face turned bright red and Rosie giggled again. It seemed that Luke had competition for the lovely Morwen.

"Morwen is well and every day grows in grace," was Esram's rather strange reply.

"She always was very close to Salvis." Luke's reply was even more strange.

"We turn off here," said Holly, breaking into Luke's thoughts, and she led them down a narrow cobbled path. When the path turned sharply to the right, they were facing a wide bay surrounded by dark cliffs and jagged rocks. There was no sand, neither was there any shallow water, only the rocks, almost like a harbour, and a long, narrow pier. Gulls and cormorants screamed to the wind as they dipped and dived after fish and all the while the ocean crashed in mighty waves over the rocks and the pier.

"This is the Bay of Perils," Holly told them. "Boats cannot really sail from here, although sometimes when the tide is on the turn and the sea calmer, some fishing boats do leave from the pier, for there are many fish to be caught in these waters, and some men will take the risk to catch the fish."

"It's wild!" Luke breathed. "I've never seen the sea so wild! Not even in Cornwall!"

"Is that where you come from?" Holly asked, leading the way over the rocks, confident of where she was going. She had obviously been here many times before.

"Yes," Luke nodded. "It's a place in England."

Holly shrugged. "I never heard of that, either. I only know Karensa... Be careful here!"

They negotiated a slippery rock and then they sat down, pulling their cloaks around them for warmth.

"I wish I'd got my fleece," Rosie complained. "What happened to our clothes, Holly?"

Holly shrugged. Rosie was sure she knew the answer but she was not going to tell them.

Rosie pointed to a place at the end of the narrow, stone pier, to where some broken fishing nets had been hung to dry.

"Are those gulls? They've got trapped in the nets, haven't they? We've got to help them!"

She jumped to her feet, but Holly pulled her back down. "This is called the Bay of Perils for a reason. The water is deep and the currents and the waves make it very dangerous. Even now the waves are crashing right over the pier. It is not safe to go out that far!"

"We can't just leave them," Rosie protested. "We have to set them free. Luke, have you got your pocket knife with you?"

"Of course not! I don't carry it round with me!"

"Yes, you do!"

Esram produced a small fishing knife which he

gave to Luke, who turned it over in his hand.

"It's been a long time since I saw one of these," he pondered.

"Give it to me," said Rosie. "I'll free them. I'm not afraid... Well, not much!"

Luke grinned and gave her a sideways glance as if to say, 'See, you're as brave as anyone else.'

"You'll need help," he said out loud.

"We shall all go," Esram decided. "Should one of us be swept over, there will be three others to pull them out."

Rosie tried not to look at the heaving water. Rosie was not a very strong swimmer.

Slowly, they edged along the pier, holding tightly to one another each time the spray crashed over them. The stones were slippery and made their journey twice as hazardous.

When they reached the nets, Luke got down on his stomach and leant over the edge, with Esram, who was bigger and stronger, holding his legs. He hacked away at the nets until the last of the birds had been set free.

When they were safely back on the shore, they lay back, cold, wet and strangely afraid, now that the danger was over.

As they sat on the rocks, the entire colony of sea birds surrounded them, circling and squalling, the pale sun golden on their white wings.

"Luke, they've come to say thank you!" Rosie cried. She remembered that on Karensa, those people who belonged to the King could understand the animal kingdom.

It was a moment to cherish.

When the gulls finally left them, their cries lost in

the crashing of the ocean, Esram got to his feet.

"There is something I must say. Luke, Rosie, I know what you think of me. You must hate me for the way my uncle treated Petroc and his family."

"We don't *hate* you," said Luke.

"I think you do, Luke," Esram replied gently. "If I was you, so would I... except that the King does not like us to hate anyone, no matter what they have done. Petroc was like a brother to you and... and... when we lived in Bellum's castle, I was unkind to Petroc many times. Petroc and Morwen have forgiven me. I cannot change what has been done. Will you forgive me, too?"

Holly looked embarrassed. Rosie stood up and threw her arms around Esram. Rosie always had a soft heart.

"Oh Esram, of course we can forgive you!"

"What about you, Luke?"

Luke sat where he was and stared at the waves, crashing against the rocks. He knew he should forgive. He knew it was right to forgive.

"Petroc was the best friend I ever had," he said, then added, ungraciously, "I'll try to forgive you."

Holly opened her mouth to voice her opinion but before she could do so, they were joined by someone else; Lindis, Tomas' daughter, had come to meet them. Rosie took one look at the pretty, dark-haired girl and instantly disliked her. She knew beyond any doubt that Lindis, no matter how friendly she might seem, belonged to Lord Bellum.

Chapter 10

A mighty work

Tomas lived on the edge of the town, in a square house with a large garden. It was the biggest house in the town, but it was not a castle or a palace, so no-one was more surprised than Tomas to be told by his wife that an important visitor waited to see him in the dining room.

Lord Bellum was dressed in black velvet trimmed with gold and the black steel sword at his side was encased in a golden scabbard encrusted with many rare jewels. His presence brooded over the room like a dark shadow.

Tomas fell to his knees and Bellum did not tell him to get up because Tomas was exactly where Bellum liked to see his servants.

"May I offer you refreshment, lord?" Tomas asked from his place on the floor.

"Your wife has already done that and I have refused," Bellum replied coldly. "I have come here because I have seen that you are not completing the task I set you."

"How so, lord?" Tomas protested. "It is going well. I have made sure the people have everything they need. How is my task not being fulfilled?"

"The people are beginning to listen to Carrik!"

"Yes, but they have no desire to return to the King. Lindis persuaded the children not to listen to

Esram and I stopped Carrik when he spoke on the market square. All is well."

A strange, growl-like sound came from Bellum's throat.

"All is not well! I will decide what is well, Tomas, not you! You will do as you are told! The people are curious, Tomas. Their interest is aroused. Do you think I would have come to your house if all was well? Carrik and the boy, Esram, must be silenced."

"But lord, there is nothing more we can do to stop them. The new order in the town states that all men and women have freedom of speech."

"Oh, there is," Lord Bellum told him softly. "Tomas, there is a lot more we can do. I will not have my plans thwarted in this way. My will shall be obeyed!"

Lindis, after spoiling their day, left early for home. Rosie's uneasy feeling about her grew stronger when Lindis took Esram and Holly to one side, whispering to them so that Luke and Rosie could not hear.

She began to feel more and more that Lindis was not to be trusted and she said as much to Luke.

"You imagine things, sister," he replied, speaking in the island way, which he knew would annoy her. "Have you not forgiven Esram? Is this all your for-giveness is worth?"

"No," she protested. "My forgiveness is real, but... but, Lindis... I don't feel Lindis is our friend."

Luke shrugged. "She seems OK to me." Now he sounded like himself again. "Actually, Rosie, I think Lindis is cool. Actually, I think she's mega cool."

Before Rosie had time to reply, Esram and Holly came over to them.

"Our clothes seem dry now," Esram said. "Before we go back to the town, Holly and me, we have something to ask of you both."

"Something very important," Holly added.

"Luke, Rosie," Esram went on, "I believe the King sent you to us. Will you come with us and meet some of our friends?"

"I don't see why not," replied Luke, wondering why they thought it so important.

"We can't show you where we meet unless you join us," Holly explained. "It is secret. Some of our friends' parents would stop them if they knew we met in this way. It is hard to explain. We shall have to cover your eyes so you cannot tell where you are going."

"I'm not sure..." Rosie didn't like the sound of this. They could be taken anywhere.

"Holly, we agreed that there was no need for that," Esram argued. "Luke was Petroc's friend and can be trusted."

"Yes, but –"

Luke's better nature took over at last. "It doesn't matter," he said quietly. "If that is what you want, Holly, then that's what we shall do." He gave Rosie's hand a squeeze.

So they allowed Esram and Holly to tie scarves over their eyes and lead them away. Luke felt very foolish and hoped no-one would see them, but they seemed to be walking away from the town. After a little while they were guided through a door and the scarves were taken from their eyes.

They blinked in the sudden light. They were in a

disused barn built of rough stone and furnished with bales of hay and an old table and chairs. In the barn, staring at them curiously, were about ten children of different ages. Rosie was dismayed to see Lindis among them.

A wiry, black-haired boy stepped forward. "Welcome. I am Jay. Esram has asked us to meet you, for he believes you have been brought here for a purpose. You can sit down."

There didn't seem to be any chairs left, so Luke and Rosie sat on some hay on the floor.

"What do you want?" asked Luke, still not trusting Esram.

Rosie added, "Who are you? Why are we here?"

Jay let Esram speak for them all. "These are the children of the town who have realised that the Guardians cannot supply everything. They need to hear about Salvis, and about the King."

"Why can't you tell them?" asked Luke.

"I can tell them only so much, for I didn't know Lord Salvis as you knew him. I have asked the King to send help and I believe he sent you."

"We know we have an empty place in our hearts," Jay explained. "We want that place to be filled. When the Guardians took over the town, they said they brought us a new morning. Well, we know there is more we need, so we are looking for a Second Morning to dawn. We are called the Children of the Second Morning."

Luke and Rosie stared at the healthy, well fed children who seemed to have everything they desired.

"Look at their eyes, Luke," Rosie whispered. "Their eyes are unhappy. They have sadness in their eyes. We must help them. I think that is why we came, or part of it. We have to tell them all we know about Salvis."

"We would need a lifetime to do that," he replied. "But we do have to help them. We need to tell them what Salvis was really like. You saw him first. You start."

Silence fell as Rosie began to speak. Time stood still for Luke and Rosie, as long-lost memories, sweet and filled with tears, returned.

"I first met Salvis," she began, "at a really sad time. I had nowhere to stay and no-one to turn to. As soon as I looked at Salvis, I stopped being afraid."

"What did Salvis look like?" Holly asked eagerly, her bossiness forgotten.

"Oh, he was tall, and a bit thin. He had dark brown eyes that were very kind. He didn't have a beard and his hair was a light brown colour and parted in the middle. He took me to a place I would be safe... Luke, you tell the rest."

For the first time in months, Luke gave memories of Salvis the freedom of his heart.

"When he spoke it was as though... as though all things were right and would come right. He was kind, yet he had a power we couldn't understand. When he died it was as though... as though we... we died with him..."

The silence was broken by a harsh cry from Lindis. "Why did he die? I'll tell you why! He couldn't even be bothered to fight! Bellum killed him! And where were you, when that happened? I heard his army ran away!"

Luke knew that it was time for the truth to be

told, no matter how much it hurt.

"I did follow him, right into Bellum's castle, but... but I got scared. I pretended I never knew him, then I ran away."

Luke's voice faded and Rosie took up the story again.

"But it wasn't the end! Salvis lives again! A few days later, we met him on the beach."

"What did he say to you?" Esram asked curiously. "Was he angry because you ran away?"

Luke looked at the floor. "No, he forgave me," he whispered. "I needed to be forgiven, too, Esram. And... and I have to forgive you."

Again the silence was broken by Lindis.

"How can we believe this? Dead people do not come alive again. They do not!"

Rosie caught her eye and Lindis looked away, but not before Rosie had recognised Lord Bellum's power in the girl. Rosie spoke silently to Salvis. *Oh, Salvis, please, please send help! We need your help!*

The barn was strangely quiet. The air was so heavy that it pressed down on their shoulders.

"Oh Luke," Rosie whispered, "Salvis is here."

"I know," he whispered back. "You're crying." He didn't know his own face was wet with tears.

The silence became more intense. Esram began to speak softly in words of ancient days, the words that he had received from the King.

"I don't know what to do," Luke murmured.

Again Lindis disturbed them. With a cry, she rushed out of the barn, declaring that they were all mad.

The silence continued.

"What shall we do?" Holly sobbed desperately. "We want to know Salvis like you, but what shall we do? What shall we do, Rosie?"

Rosie knelt down in front of Holly. She took the older girl's hands in her own. "You must tell the King you're sorry for turning away from him, and then ask the Lord to be your lord, for ever."

Without any hesitation or embarrassment, Holly obeyed. Jay, who by now was also in tears, followed her. One by one, each of the children offered their lives to their rightful King.

"Oh, Luke, this is why we came back," Rosie breathed.

Her brother didn't reply. He couldn't speak. The sense of the King's son being with them was so great.

"I never felt like this before!" Holly cried. "I never knew it felt like this!"

"It's like being a new person!" Jay echoed.

"I feel as though I've known the Lord for ever!"

"Everything looks different!"

"The empty place in my heart... it is filled!"

"And mine!"

"It was so easy!"

"This is what we were looking for! This is the Second Morning! We have found the Second Morning!"

They were all so excited that by the time they left the barn, the sky was streaked with pale crimson as the sun faded into the mist.

With glorious colours, the sky was praising the King.

The trees praised the King too, their bare branches bowing low before him.

The stream in the meadow sang a song to praise the King as it chattered over the stones.

The granite clad moors praised the King with their ancient strength.

The field creatures praised the King as they scurried about their business without fear.

The sea crashed wildly against the rocks in the Bay of Perils and praised the King with a loud voice.

The wild grasses praised the King as they swayed to the music of the wind.

The wind praised the King as it sighed across the meadows.

Far away in the Dark Forest, the stag and the deer lifted their heads to praise the King.

On the other side of the island, Petroc and Morwen praised the King who had restored their farm.

In the deep water, dolphins raced with rainbows and praised the King, leaping high through the waves.

Sea birds praised the King with plaintive cries as they dived across the rocks.

Eagles praised the King as they soared above the moor.

From north to south and east to west, Karensa praised the King.

Holly praised the King because the hurt for her mother did not hurt so much any more.

Luke and Rosie praised the King with new words.

Esram praised the King who had heard his cry and this day had done a mighty work in their lives.

Chapter 11

"The Father of Lies"

Jay's farm was a little way outside the town, and the path was narrow, so Holly and Rosie walked in front of the boys. Rosie had composed a song for the Children of the Second Morning, and she and Holly sang it together.

"The Children of the Second Morning,
Awaiting the New Day's dawning.

Children against the night,
Seeking the Spirit's light.
Children prepared to fight,
Standing for truth and right.

We're the Children of the Second Morning,
Hearts ready for the New Day's dawning."

"I like that," said Holly, slipping her hand through Rosie's arm in a gesture of friendship. "That can be the Children's special song, their anthem. Do you make up lots of songs, Rosie?"

"Well, a few," Rosie said modestly. "I made one up for our youth group at church."

"What's church?"

Rosie hesitated. "Oh, it's a place we go," she said finally. Holly seemed satisfied with that.

She was suddenly aware that Holly was staring at her.

"What's the matter?" she laughed. "Have I got a spot?"

Holly's cheeks turned pink. "I just... I wish... I would love to be pretty, Rosie, like you!"

It was Rosie's turn to be embarrassed. "I'm not pretty! I'm ordinary!"

"You are! You have lovely curly hair and big eyes. My hair is straight and my eyes are really small!"

Holly sounded as though she was close to tears and Rosie felt sorry for her.

"You could do more with your hair," she said practically. "If you had a fringe, maybe your eyes would look bigger? Will you let me do it?"

"I'll see... Shall we sing again?"

They began the new song, but almost at once the notes turned into screams, for as they rounded the next bend in the path, a dark shape loomed over them and they were scooped high into the air...

Luke and Esram walked behind them, busy forming their own friendship. Now that Luke had made up his mind to forgive Esram, he found that he really liked the older boy. Esram had a sense of humour and did not mind laughing at himself. He bore no resentment that it was Luke and Rosie, not himself, who had led the children to the King.

Luke told him a little of his own world, of TV and computers and cars. Esram didn't seem to understand and couldn't grasp the idea of travelling in a box with four rubber wheels.

"Do you never walk, then?" he asked.

"Well, yes, sometimes. We walk to keep healthy."

"Why not walk anyway then, and do away with the cars? That would make more sense. Why –"

His words were cut short by loud screams from the girls and Luke and Esram raced to catch them up.

Luke reached them first and came face to face with Lord Bellum.

Bellum's head was thrown back in laughter and he had Rosie under one arm and Holly under the other. Both girls were screaming, but Rosie kept still and screamed, whereas Holly was kicking and fighting.

A little way off, Bellum's fine black horse stood waiting, that very same horse which had once carried Luke to the King's Palace. They had travelled faster than the wind. The ride had been thrilling. Luke thought about it now.

But he had forgotten how fierce the dark-haired lord could be, had forgotten his giant-like frame and black eyes. Luke was also aware that there was something about Lord Bellum that fascinated people, yet was deeply repulsive.

Bellum laughed in a musical voice, which was part of his attraction.

"Greetings, Luke! I had heard you were back on Karensa. I have already met your sister!"

He gave Rosie a rough shake so that she wailed with terror.

Luke stepped forward. "Leave her alone, Bellum! Set her down! Set them both down!"

"Who commands me?" Bellum cried, still laughing in a mocking way. "Do you command me, Luke? You? You could not even remain loyal to Salvis! You ran away and let him die on his own! Who are you to command me?"

Luke, still filled with the power Salvis had given him and still very aware of his presence, faced the dark-haired lord and was not afraid.

"I'm a follower of Lord Salvis, that's who I am, Bellum! Now set them both down!"

No-one was more surprised than Luke when Bellum obeyed and dropped the two girls. They landed in a heap at Luke's feet, and the screams stopped.

They scrambled up, more frightened than hurt, and Bellum turned his attention to Esram.

"Carrik's boy! You chose a farm rather than my castle, Esram. Do you never regret it?"

"No, never," Esram told him in a strong voice. Salvis had left his power with him, too.

"You will," Bellum assured him. "Do you think you will win the people here for the King, Esram? Well, you will not. They will never leave the protection of the Guardians. They will not want to hear about your King." He reached out a hand and began to stroke his horse's neck. "Esram, there is no King! No-one lives in the Royal Palace any more. Salvis is not there. He is dead and remains dead."

Rosie found her voice. "Salvis isn't dead! You're telling lies, Bellum!"

Bellum shrugged carelessly. "Whatever. It does not matter. You will find out the truth for yourselves. As for you, Luke, I will tell you this. You will never again see your so-called friends, Petroc and Morwen, and without my help, you will never return to Poldawn."

Without warning, Luke felt laughter rising in his throat. The idea that they would need help from the King's enemy to get home was so ridiculous that he simply had to laugh.

Lord Bellum sprang on his horse's back and rode off without another word.

The young people stood without speaking for a little while. Just as at the Bay of Perils when they rescued the sea birds, now that the danger was past they had time to be afraid.

"Is he always like that?" Holly asked at last.

"No," Esram shook his head and grinned. "Bellum is usually much worse. You should see him when he is really angry."

"I do not like him. I do not ever want to see him again," Holly replied.

"I believe we will see him again," Luke sighed. "He won't leave us alone now. I had forgotten what he was like."

"He said we would never see Petroc and Morwen again," said Rosie. "That was a lie. I know we shall see them one day! I feel it in my heart. Bellum is telling lies."

"Bellum always tells lies," Esram declared. "I know him the best of all of us and I know he tells lies as easily as he draws breath. He is the Father of Lies."

Holly suddenly shivered. "I want to go home. I'm afraid. I think something has happened at home. We should hurry."

She could not explain why she felt like this, but

the others picked up on her fear and they hurried back to the town as quickly as they could.

They were too late. When they reached Reuben's shop, Guardians were everywhere, inside the shop and outside the door. A crowd had gathered to watch and the house was in turmoil.

They pushed to the front of the crowd and looked past the Guardians into the shop. Reuben was lying by his work bench as though dead, and blood was seeping from a wound to his head and trickling across the floor.

Chapter 12

"Who would hate me so?"

Reuben stirred, moaning softly. With a cry of fear, Holly pushed her way through the group of Guardians who were standing in the shop doorway. The soldiers were so surprised that they failed to stop her.

"This is my house!" she stormed. "That is my father, lying on the floor! Let me come in! You have no right to keep me away from my own home. It is not lawful!"

The Guardians were so bound up with keeping the law of the town that they allowed her to enter.

Unable to hold back her tears, she ran over to Reuben and fell on her knees by his side.

"Oh, Father, I thought you... it looked like you were dead... First Mother, then you... I could not bear it if you left me, too! Are you badly hurt?"

Rosie, always soft hearted, started to cry with her. This was the real Holly and the real Holly must have been hurting deep inside and hiding her pain for so long by pretending that she was unfeeling and bossy. In that way she could always be in control. It was her shield against pain.

Reuben struggled into a sitting position, holding his head. His naturally rosy face turned deathly white as the trickle of blood from his head became a steady flow.

"You Guardians, you have to let my friends come in!" Holly commanded, once again taking charge. "This is their home, too. Your own law says you have to protect our homes. Rosie, get some water and a cloth. And a bandage, we shall need a bandage. We must stop the bleeding. Esram, Luke, help my father into a chair. Oh, hurry, all of you, you are wasting time!"

Grudgingly, the Guardians moved aside to let the other young people pass and they each hurried to do as they were told. Soon Reuben was looking a little better and he sat in his favourite chair while Rosie and Holly bandaged his wound.

"What happened, Father?" Holly whispered. "The shop... the shop is wrecked!"

Rosie heard what Holly said and looked around. Everything in the shop that could be smashed, had been smashed. Pots of glue had been overturned. Reuben's best leathers had all been slashed with a knife and his wooden lasts must surely be beyond repair. In the back room, a pot of soup had been simmering on the range and this was now upset all over the floor so that warm soup was running everywhere. On the settle, the cushions so lovingly made by Holly's mother had been ripped open, the feathers strewn on the floor.

One name came into Rosie's mind: Lindis. She had left the meeting in an outburst of temper. She could easily have told her father what was happening in Jay's barn.

Reuben groaned. "Oh, my daughter, I cannot recall what happened. I saw a dark shape coming towards me but that is all I saw."

"Didn't you see the face?" asked Luke, thinking

of how his favourite TV detective would behave.

"Well, I believe I did see him, but.. but I cannot remember now. Oh, who would do this to me? Who would hate me so?"

The thought that someone could hate him so much was more than Reuben could bear for he had never hurt anyone. He covered his face with his hands, repeating over and over, "Who would hate me so?"

Rosie's lip trembled again. She liked Reuben. He had been so kind to them and he really wanted to know about the King. She put her own small hand over his gnarled fingers.

"Don't worry about the mess. You must rest now. We shall clear all the mess away while you are lying down. When you get up, it will all be clean."

The others voiced their agreement.

"Not replaced!" Reuben cried, now even more distressed. "Look at the damage this has caused. It will cost me my life's savings to replace what has been destroyed."

Such attacks were commonplace in Luke's world. He nearly said as much, but wisely changed his mind.

One of the Guardians came up to them. Until now the soldiers had been watching without becoming involved.

"Friend Reuben, can you tell us nothing of what happened? The people who did this need to be punished to fulfil the requirements of Guardian law."

"No," Reuben sighed. "Nothing at all. I may have seen who did this, but if so, then it has gone from my mind."

Suddenly Esram noticed that Carrik was missing. "Where is my uncle? Why is he not here?"

Reuben looked blank. Another of the Guardians told them that he had seen Carrik leaving the shop just before they had been called to the scene.

"He was in a great hurry," he added. "Maybe it was he who did this to you, Reuben?"

Esram protested. "My uncle would not do such a thing!"

Luke said nothing. Recollections of the bad things that Carrik had done to them in the past sneaked into his mind.

The first Guardian bent down and picked up a gilt clasp from the place where Reuben had been lying.

"Does this not belong to the stranger, Carrik?" he said. "He must have dropped it when he hit Reuben."

"That could have been dropped at any time," Esram cried. "I know my uncle would not do this. Reuben, he was your friend!"

At that very moment Carrik chose to return. He stood in the shop doorway, regarding the scene but not saying a word.

"It was him, I know it!" said the second Guardian. "He has been trouble ever since he arrived in the town. All this talk about the King! We do not want to know about the King!"

"No!" Esram insisted. "Uncle Carrik is Reuben's friend!"

"Some friend!" the man sneered. "Arrest him!"

Two more Guardians moved forward and took hold of Carrik's arms, holding him fast.

Luke's sense of right and wrong prompted him to

join in.

"You can't do this!" he told them. "You can't arrest him without evidence! It's not legal!"

The man held out the gilt clasp. "This is all the evidence we need."

"That's not proper evidence! That could have fallen on the floor at any time. It's not right to arrest someone without proper evidence. It wouldn't happen in my world! You'd need a good reason to arrest someone!"

Rosie echoed his words, but their protests were met by laughter.

"You are not in your world now," they were told. "You are on the island of Karensa and here in the town we have our own laws, the laws that the Guardians have made for the benefit of the people and the good keeping of all. They are not your laws and they are not the King's laws either!"

As the Guardians led Carrik off, Esram sprang forward and tried to push them away.

"No, you cannot do this! My uncle is innocent!"

Carrik stopped him, speaking for the first time. "You cannot win in this way," he told him gently. "If I am to go to prison, then I shall go to prison. You will only bring trouble on yourself by behaving in this way. You cannot help me, nephew. Only one person can help me."

"But you are innocent!"

"I know that. So do you. So does the King, remember that. Salvis has promised never to leave us. He will send help from the King. Now, Esram, stand back and let the Guardians do their work. Soon, Reuben will remember who it really was who hurt him, and then I shall go free. Until that day, he is a kind man and he will look after you all."

Esram was hardly listening. He desperately tried to pull the Guardians away from Carrik, but one of them, seemingly without any effort at all, hit him with the back of his hand so that the youth was sent sprawling into the mess of cold soup on the floor.

The men laughed. Esram tried to get up, but the floor was slippery and he felt dizzy. By the time he managed to get to his feet, the Guardians had left, taking Carrik with them.

Holly's face turned red, then white with anger. She glared at Luke and Rosie.

"So this is what belonging to the King gets for us! Well, you can keep your King and his dead son, too!" She ran upstairs to throw herself on her bed, leaving Luke, Rosie and Esram to clear up the mess.

Rosie pulled a slice of carrot from Esram's hair.

"How can this be?" she whispered. "It was so good... all the children, turning to the King... Now this!"

"It is *because* the children decided to follow Salvis," Esram told her. "This has Bellum's hand on it, I know it. He will not risk losing his power over the town."

Now that the excitement was over, the crowd outside the shop began to move away, and with them went Tomas, the leader of the Guardians, and his daughter, Lindis.

Tomas was smiling and Lindis was fingering a new gold chain at her throat, a gift from Lord Bellum.

Chapter 13
The trial

When they had gone, the house seemed strangely quiet; not the peaceful stillness that the children had encountered in the barn, but a confused, disturbing quiet, broken only by the muffled sound of Holly sobbing in her room upstairs.

Esram said, "Someone should go to her," and he looked hopefully at Rosie.

She nodded. "I'll go," and the boys looked relieved.

She found Holly lying face down on her bed, her thin shoulders shaking uncontrollably. When she heard Rosie, she turned over on to her back. Her face was red and blotchy and her eyes were swollen with tears.

Rosie felt a rush of sympathy for her. "Oh Holly," was all she said, then she sat with the older girl and held her until she stopped crying.

"We must clear up," Holly sighed at last, wiping her eyes.

"No, you stay here," Rosie said kindly. "Or better still, persuade your father to go to bed. He should rest, but he wants to sit in his chair."

"Yes," Holly agreed in a flat, defeated sort of voice. "Yes, of course, that is what I shall do."

When they went downstairs, the boys had already made a start on the clearing up. They had found a bar of washing soda and the kitchen was now clean, but Reuben still sat in his favourite chair, looking white and dazed.

Holly took hold of his hand. "Father, you must rest. You must go to bed. Come with me, please."

Reuben's eyes flickered, but they rested, not on Holly who was kneeling by his side, but on Esram.

"Who would hate me so?" was all he would say.

Esram started to say that whoever it was, it was not his Uncle Carrik. Seeing how confused Reuben was, he thought better of it, and Holly was able to gently lead her father to his room.

When she came down again, she told them that he was getting ready for bed.

"He needs broth, though," she added. "We have none. That was our supper. We have nothing to eat at all."

Even as she spoke, there was a knock on the door. Luke shrugged off a sudden moment of fear and went to see who it was. He was surprised to see Lindis standing at the door, a laden basket over her arm.

"I have brought food, a gift from my father, Tomas. The Guardians will not see anyone go hungry. Can I come in?"

"Yes... yes, come in," Luke stammered, too confused to know what to do.

Lindis looked around her. "What a mess! Holly, I told you that the King would not look after you as well as the Guardians! Did I not say?"

Holly didn't answer. It was obvious that a battle was raging in Holly's heart.

"Here is new bread for you, and a side of cold meat, and apple pie. Oh, and a dish of broth for Reuben. He should have something light."

Rosie tried to suppress a shudder as their hands touched. Lindis saw the shudder and moved closer to her, whispering so that only Rosie could hear.

"You know me, Rosie, do you not? The others do not know me, but you do?"

Rosie nodded. She looked Lindis in the eye and was now certain of who this nut-brown maid served.

"So, we know each other," Lindis continued. "You and I, Rosie, shall never be friends."

Her words carried a threat, but Rosie reminded herself that the King's power was with her and she was not afraid.

"Oh," Lindis looked up, her face innocent. "Oh, I forgot. My father said to tell you that Carrik is to stand trial the day after tomorrow at the Guardians' House and you are all commanded to be there. Now, I must go."

The shop door shut behind her and they were left staring at the basket of food. Rosie did not want to eat it, but they had nothing else in the house and she was very hungry.

It seemed as though the whole town had come to Carrik's trial, which reminded Luke of a military court he had once seen on TV. On one side of the hall sat the Guardians, each dressed in their uniform of grey tunic and dark blue cloak. Opposite them sat the townspeople and it was to these seats that Reuben and the children were shown. At the end of the hall, in the judge's seat, was Tomas, and facing that seat was a low stool for the accused.

Yesterday had been a strange day. Esram hardly

spoke to anyone, but stayed in his room on his own, probably sharing his thoughts with Salvis. Luke could not help feeling sorry for Esram. The only family he had was Carrik, and Carrik had been taken away. Holly had spent the day looking after Reuben, who was still very dazed. She made it plain that she had no time for Luke or Rosie. As for Rosie, she went to the shop for food and cooked the supper, all on her own. Luke and Rosie had quarrelled about Lindis and had only just started speaking to each other again.

When Carrik was led in by two Guardians, they were all surprised to see that he had been treated well. He was wearing clean clothes and his hair was washed and combed. Carrik had never treated his own prisoners so well.

He was told to sit on the low stool and as Tomas stood up, a respectful silence fell.

"Let the trial commence. Who represents the Guardians?"

A tall, grey-haired man stepped forward. He was dressed like the other Guardians, except for a scarlet sash around his waist.

"Sir, I am that officer."

"Who speaks for the prisoner?"

Carrik stood up. His voice was steady and sure. "I shall speak for myself, sir. I am represented by the rightful King of Karensa and by his son, Lord Salvis."

Rosie gave a little clap of her hands. Many people in the hall were laughing, but Luke thought Carrik was brave. Esram said nothing, but he was proud of his uncle.

So the trial began and one by one, people were

questioned. Carrik explained that he had only left the house to look for the children, who were very late coming home. It was while he was away from the shop that the raid had taken place.

Reuben was still confused and couldn't remember any more than he had on that night.

Finally, the clasp was produced and the officer stated that the clasp was found right next to Reuben and this proved Carrik's guilt.

"Not so, sir," Carrik protested. "I lost the clasp that very morning, in the market square. Someone must have picked it up and placed it where they knew I should be blamed."

This was greeted by a great outburst of laughter, not least from Tomas, who as Carrik's judge was not supposed to have an opinion of his own.

Esram looked dismayed. It was very clear which way the trial was going. Tomas held up his hand for silence but he did so in a way which showed that really, he agreed.

"There can be no question of this man's guilt. He was seen leaving the house just before the raid happened. He must have returned and taken our good friend Reuben by surprise. If that is not proof enough, his clasp was found by Reuben's side, right where he lay. These two things prove that Carrik is guilty. While our friend Reuben was offering him hospitality, he repaid him by wrecking our friend's home. He deserves to be kept in prison until the court decides he may go free."

"No!" Esram leapt to his feet. "This is not justice! There is no justice here at all!"

Although Luke tried to hold him back, he was not quick enough. Esram left his seat and ran to where his uncle sat in the centre of the hall.

"Silence! Return to your place!" Tomas thundered.

"I will not, sir. This court is a mockery! It would seem to me that it is not my uncle who should be on trial but another in this hall!"

There could be no doubt that he meant Tomas, and the leader of the Guardians knew this too. His handsome face contorted with rage.

"Very well, if this youth is so concerned, then he shall share his uncle's punishment. Carrik will have a companion for his long stay in prison." He gave a short laugh. "That is well, for now he will not be lonely! Guardians, take them both away! They shall stay in prison until their lesson has been truly learnt."

Rosie clutched her brother's arm. "Luke! They can't do this! It's not right!"

"They've done it," he replied grimly as they watched Esram, his face white and scared, being dragged from the hall with Carrik. "They've won, Rosie. I can't believe it! Tomas has won! What is the King doing? Where is he now?"

"No," Rosie murmured softly. "Luke, Tomas has not won. Only a battle. Remember how we thought Bellum had won when he killed Salvis? Yet Salvis won in the end. Salvis has promised never to leave us. Salvis will be true to his word."

When they returned to the boot-maker's shop, Reuben asked them to sit down around the large kitchen table.

"Poor Esram!" Rosie exclaimed. "He has done nothing wrong at all and yet he is to be punished.

The Guardians could keep them in prison for years!"

"Do you want us to leave, Reuben?" Luke asked, aware of Reuben's change in attitude. "You do not have to offer us a home. We are not your responsibility any more."

"I shall not turn you away," Reuben said sternly. "You are not to blame for what has happened to me, but at the same time it is true that you have brought trouble upon us with all your talk about the King. You may continue to stay here, but you will no longer be my guests. I shall need help now that I have to begin again and there will be too much work for Holly to do on her own. I must rebuild my business and that will leave me no time for household chores. You must both work to earn your meals and lodgings."

"We are not afraid of work," said Luke. The first time they had come to Karensa, both he and Rosie had learnt about hard work. "We can both work, Reuben."

"Sir," Reuben corrected him. "You should call me 'sir', I think... Yes, that would be best."

He seemed distressed and Rosie would have loved to offer him words of comfort, but she could not. Reuben had made it plain that he was only helping them from human kindness. He no longer wanted to be their friend.

Holly, too, spoke to them in a cold voice. "It is well that you are not afraid of work, Luke. You can start by chopping wood for the range. It is stacked in the yard. Then you can sweep the shop. Rosie, there are blankets to wash. See you get them clean before you hang them out to dry. Oh, one thing more. We do not want to hear about Salvis. Not another word from either of you. Now I am going to the Bay of Perils... Lindis is waiting for me."

Chapter 14

"The King has made a way"

Almost without being noticed, the Time of Snows slipped into the Time of New Birth. From the window of their room in the Guardians' House, Esram and Carrik could see across the town to the countryside beyond, and each day they watched trees become laden with blossom, and hedgerows with wild flowers. The air was warm, and the sea, except in the Bay of Perils, gently lapped against the rocky shore.

Carrik and Esram were well looked after by the Guardians. Their room was comfortable. They each had a narrow bed with feather pillows, and only the bars at the window and the locked door reminded them that the room was a prison.

Neither could they complain about their food, which was plentiful and good. Each day they were brought fresh water to wash with and a regular change of clothes. Yet they were not free, and Esram, at least, was bored. Esram longed to be out in the open air, walking across the hills or climbing over the rocks on the beach, watching the ebb and flow of the sea. He began to wonder if Salvis really was with them, or if he had deserted them.

One good thing did come from their imprisonment. Carrik had taken Esram into his household from a sense of duty when his parents had disappeared, many years ago, but he had never been close to him. Months of sharing each other's company had given them a new understanding. Esram realised that, just like himself, Carrik had been lonely. For the first time, they really cared about each other. Each day they would share thoughts about the King as they praised him together.

One day, just after their midday meal, a surprise visitor arrived, and Esram sprang to his feet with joy.

"Luke! You have come at last!"

Luke had the grace to blush. "I didn't know you could have visitors," he explained. "Then Jay told me it was the Guardians' law that any prisoner may have one visitor each day. So I came. How... how are you both?"

"We do well enough, Luke," Carrik sighed. "We are not free, that is all."

"You will be," Luke promised. "We shall find a way to set you free. They cannot keep you here for ever!"

"We shall see," Carrik replied, smiling.

Esram added, "Tell us how you've been? Is Reuben looking after you and Rosie?"

"Well, yes, he is, but not as he was before. Now we have to work for him, but we don't mind really. He has a kind heart and gives us time to ourselves each afternoon, so it's not so bad. He's not friendly any more, though."

"Does he remember what happened?" Carrik wanted to know.

"No, not a thing. And he doesn't want to hear

about Salvis any more, either."

"Many do, though," Esram said mysteriously.

"What do you mean?"

Esram's eyes shone with excitement. "As you said, Luke, we are allowed one visitor each day, and they are coming! The people from the town are coming to see us! They made fun of us when they were with the crowd, but one by one and alone, they are listening to what we have to say about the King!"

"They do not have to fear their neighbours' mockery when they are on their own," Carrik explained.

"You mean people are coming here? To the prison?"

"Yes, Luke," Carrik replied. "If Bellum thought that locking us away would stop us, he was wrong. The opposite has happened. The King has made a way for us to talk to the people where there seemed to be no way at all."

"Rosie was right," said Luke. "She said we had only lost one battle, not the war."

Carrik threw back his head and laughed loudly. "Your sister is wise beyond her years! We have not lost the war, Luke! We cannot lose the war! The last battle has already been fought and won! The outcome has been decided. The battle was won the moment Salvis gave his own life to take the punishment for our disobedience. Now all that is left for us to do is to win people back to the King, and that is the task we have been given. You and Rosie must play your part, too. Are the Children of the Second Morning still meeting?"

His words were thrilling, but Luke looked

questioningly at Esram, who nodded. "I told Uncle Carrik about the children and how they had turned to the King."

"Well then, yes, they are still meeting. They want to hear more and more about Salvis and all the things he did. Only... Holly will not come any more. She doesn't want to know."

"She will," said Carrik softly. "She is hurting, Luke, but now that she has accepted the King as her rightful Lord, Salvis will not let her go."

Luke was silent. How could this gentle man be the same Carrik who had delighted in tormenting the King's people? Carrik must have guessed what he was thinking.

"Oh yes, Luke, we all have to change," he told him, and Luke's face turned red, because there had been a time when he, too, had needed to change.

"How is Rosie?" said Esram, eager to catch up with the news. "Have you heard anything about Petroc, or Morwen?"

Esram still blushed at the thought of Morwen, and Luke felt unreasonably annoyed with him.

"Nothing from Petroc," he replied curtly. "Rosie is all right, but she misses Holly being friends. Holly spends all her time with Lindis now."

"She should be careful of Lindis," Esram said thoughtfully. "Do not trust her, Luke."

So Esram agreed with Rosie about Tomas' daughter?

"Lindis is OK," he muttered half-heartedly, beginning to think that he might be wrong after all.

A sound outside the door told them that it was time for visitors to go.

"We shall get you out," Luke whispered. "One

way or another, we'll get you out of here. I promise."

It was a rash promise and Carrik and Esram knew it.

"That may not be the King's will," Carrik said quickly, before the Guardian opened the door. "In here we are able to tell people about Salvis and that is the reason we came to the far side of the island. I believe with all my heart that you and Rosie should think more about helping the Children of the Second Morning than about getting us out of prison. The King will do that at the right time. I believe that is what the King wants you to do. I believe that the children are the reason that you have both been brought back to Karensa."

After Luke had gone and the door was locked again, Esram's mood changed.

"Do you think we shall have to stay here long, Uncle?" he sighed, looking longingly at the world outside.

Carrik placed a hand on his nephew's fair head. "I do not know," he said honestly. "We shall stay for as long as the King needs us to stay. If it helps, I remind myself that other prisoners in the past were not treated as well as us."

"You mean Petroc?"

"I mean Petroc. Others, too."

"Well, we are both guilty there," Esram sighed. "We were both cruel to Petroc."

"Guilty, yes," said Carrik. "But forgiven, Esram. You must never forget that both Petroc and Salvis have forgiven us. Come, nephew, be brave. Do not lose heart. The King knows where we are and I am sure he will not forget us, for is it not his work we are doing?"

In Jay's barn, Rosie finished telling the story about how Lord Salvis had once healed a little girl who could not speak, and the Children of the Second Morning were sprawled around her. The children's eyes no longer looked sad. They shone brighter than the brightest stars.

The young people did not believe that Carrik had attacked Reuben. Now they had asked Salvis into their lives, they knew Carrik could not have done such a thing.

"I wish I had known Lord Salvis," Jay sighed.

"You do know him," Rosie told him.

Jay's rather solemn face suddenly broke into a wide smile. "Yes, we do know him now," he agreed. "And I want to know him more. More and more and more."

"Not right now you don't," Luke grinned. "We have to get back so that Rosie can cook supper, then maybe tonight she won't spoil it?"

He was only teasing her, but Rosie was tired. She had been scrubbing floors all morning and in the afternoon Luke had left her on her own while he went to visit Carrik and Esram. Rosie didn't often feel sorry for herself, but right now her tiredness got the better of her, and without a word to anyone, she stormed away. She knew that this was not the way Salvis would want her to behave, but she didn't care.

Rosie wanted to go home. Not to the town. Not even to the other side of the island, the familiar places she and Luke had once known, but to her real home; to Poldawn. Rosie wanted to go home more than anything she had ever wanted for a long time.

She closed her eyes as she stood by the stile at the end of the lane.

"Oh Salvis, please, please let us go home. I hate it here. It's not like it used to be. No-one wants us. No-one likes us. They don't want to know about you. Please, please Salvis, let us go home."

Even as she spoke she knew that Salvis would not show them the way home until their work was done. They couldn't pick and choose which jobs they wanted to do for the King. It was for them to obey him. She also knew that the King's judgement was wise and he knew what was best for them. She had to trust him.

"I will do it, Lord King," she promised in a whisper. "I'm sorry. I won't let you down, but please help me."

She hadn't heard Luke come up behind her and when he put his hand on her shoulder, she jumped.

"I'm sorry, Rosie," he said. "It was a silly joke. There's nothing wrong with your cooking."

"I'm only ten! I'm doing my best!"

"I know. It's hard for both of us."

"If only Reuben was still our friend! If only Petroc and Morwen were here! I'm lonely!"

"So am I," he admitted. "I know the King has work for us to do, but, oh Rosie, so am I! I want to go home!"

Chapter 15

A river of tears

A few days later, Luke and Rosie had finished their work earlier than usual. Holly had gone out with Lindis immediately after she had washed the dishes, which was her only contribution to the housework.

It was the first really warm day, and Luke was fed up with chopping wood and sweeping the shop floor and sorting out tacks and nails. He wanted to be outside in the fresh air. Luke never liked to stay indoors for too long, and he wondered how Esram endured being locked in that small room day after day.

"Rosie, why don't we go up to the moors?" he suggested. "As high as we can go? So high we might see the whole island, even Petroc's farm?"

"Do you think it's very far?" Rosie looked out of the window to where the high moors towered, wild and lonely. They might meet Lord Bellum again. The memory of being hauled off her feet by Bellum still haunted Rosie each night before she went to sleep. She didn't want to see Lindis, either, for Lindis had made it plain that she and Rosie were enemies.

"Well, if it did turn out to be too far, we could always turn back," Luke told her.

Rosie wasn't convinced. She had encountered

Luke's "turning back" before. Luke was not a "turning back" sort of person.

"If we go, we must tell Reuben," she insisted. Luke agreed. It seemed a small price to pay for an afternoon's freedom.

Reuben did not mind them going out. He even provided bread, cold meat and goat's milk for their journey. However, he warned them to turn back home at once if the mist should come down. He must still care about them in his way.

As they left pastures, orchards and vineyards behind, the soft grass became coarse and patchy and strewn with granite rocks, around which gorse and heather thrived.

"It's getting colder," Rosie shivered, pulling her cloak around her shoulders.

"We need our fleeces. I wonder what happened to our own clothes?"

"I wonder what's happened at home? Our real home, I mean – Poldawn. I wonder how Pepper is getting on? Does she miss us, Luke? Does she even realise we've gone?"

She was doing it again! Asking him questions he could not possibly answer!

"How do I know?" he snapped. "Last time we came to Karensa, no-one even knew we'd gone. When we got home, everything was just as we left it. Time's different here."

"How long shall we have to stay?"

"Rosie! How do I know?"

His sister sighed deeply. "I wish we did know, Luke. We don't seem to be doing much here, do we? Holly doesn't like us any more. Reuben doesn't really want to look after us. It wouldn't be so bad if we knew when we were going home. Or even if we are going home at all!"

They walked a little way in silence, then Luke said, "I don't understand how Carrik could change so much, Rosie, do you? He was mega cruel! He was as bad as Lord Bellum. Yet now he's willing to give up his own freedom so that people can hear about how much the King loves them. He'd sooner stay in prison where people will listen to him than come out and have nobody interested in what he's got to say. He must really love the King."

"Maybe," Rosie replied thoughtfully, "it's because he was so bad in the past. The King had lots of bad things to forgive him, so maybe that made Carrik love him lots more?"

"Maybe."

By now they had reached the highest point and they sat on the rocks to eat the food that Reuben had given them. The last part of their long climb had been hard, but it had warmed them up and made them forget all about needing their fleeces. They were glad of the cold milk, and drank deeply.

The day was bright and clear with no sign of mist, except for the mist that was always present on Karensa at the point where the sea met the sky.

"Look behind us," Luke pointed across the island. "Rosie, you can see the battlements of Lord Bellum's castle!"

Rosie shaded her eyes. "So you can!" She shivered involuntarily. "Oh Luke, I don't ever want to go there! But if you look really hard you can see another castle, to the right of that one and just behind it!"

"I can't!"

"Yes you can! This castle has turrets of gold and pennants of silver!"

"The Royal Palace!" Luke breathed. "Rosie, we can see the Royal Palace!"

Without warning, Rosie burst into tears. Not little tears that she could hide, not gentle, feminine tears, but a river of tears that poured down her face and splashed her tunic.

Luke stared at her. "What's the matter with you?"

"I don't know... Yes, I do, I do... I do know... It's Salvis. Oh, I want to see Salvis so much it hurts inside!"

"So do I," he agreed. "And even more than Salvis, I want to see Petroc and Morwen."

As they stared sadly across the island, they saw two horses galloping towards them, one large and grey and the other smaller and brown.

"Is it the Guardians?" Rosie asked in a worried voice. "I don't want to meet them up here."

"No, it's not them," Luke said slowly. "They're coming from the other side of the island, from the direction of the Royal Palace, I think."

Rosie squealed. "It must be Salvis!"

"It's not Salvis... I think it's Lord Veritan... There are two people on the other horse, but I don't know them."

The two horses stopped at the foot of the hill. Luke was right. The rider of the big, grey horse was Veritan, Lord of the Royal Palace and the King's most loyal servant.

Splendid as ever, with his jewelled circlet and silver hair and the golden sword of truth at his side, Veritan saluted them and they waved back. Then he dismounted and helped his companions down from the other horse. He pointed to the hill.

At first Petroc and Morwen did not recognise them. Then they did. They stopped, then raced up the steep hill. "Luke? Is it you? Oh, it is, it is!" Petroc threw his arms around Luke's shoulders and they did a little dance of joy, right there on the high moors.

They stood back and took stock of each other and for a few minutes the months that had separated them were forgotten.

Luke saw a youth with shoulder-length red-gold hair and light green eyes that sparkled with excitement. Petroc had always been tall but when Luke had last seen him, he had been pale and thin. Now he was strong and healthy.

"It is me, brother," Luke replied, for they had called one another this ever since the night they had sworn brotherhood on a place called High Hill.

"Oh, Luke, how I have longed to see you again! I knew you would return! I knew you had to come back to Karensa one day!"

"I've missed you," Luke admitted. "I've missed you all, really. I've missed Karensa, too. And Salvis... But look at you, brother! The last time we were together, you were so weak and ill you couldn't even beat me at skimming pebbles."

"That was Carrik's doing; Carrik and Bellum."

Luke nodded. "Now you are a full head and shoulders taller than me. And you've grown strong!"

"You have grown, but outwards!" Petroc laughed.

It was true. Luke was quite solid for thirteen. He grinned and flexed his muscles. "Look, no fat. I'm in the school rugby team."

"Rugby team?"

"Oh, it's a game. Never mind." Luke remembered the others. He pulled away from Petroc, turning his attention to the quiet girl standing behind him.

"Morwen?"

Morwen, too, had grown. She was now as tall as Luke and her red hair was neatly plaited in a single thick braid over one shoulder. Like Petroc, she was dressed in a tunic and trousers of soft grey which suited her green eyes. Her face was still freckled, but there was a gentle beauty about her that had not been there before.

She held out her hands and for a moment they were both embarrassed because they had once been so close. The hardships they had shared meant that Luke knew Morwen very well. He had been there at the saddest time of her life and when they lived in the Bay of Dolphins, she had shared with him all her hopes and dreams. Morwen knew Luke, too. On the night Salvis died, Luke had denied he even knew him and had run away. He left Salvis to die alone. Morwen had witnessed Luke's guilt and pain afterwards.

They both blushed. Luke swallowed hard to get rid of a lump in his throat.

"Luke, I have missed you so much," she said with truthful simplicity.

He was honest, too. "I've missed you. You look

well."

It was not what he wanted to say at all and there was an awkward silence, broken by Rosie, who coughed loudly.

"Rosie!" Petroc cried. "I did not recognise you, for you are so grown up now!"

"No, I'm not. You knew it was me. You just ignored me!"

"We could not," Morwen laughed. "You would not let us forget you even if we tried. How are you, Rosie? I have missed you, too. But... but how are you both already dressed in island clothes?"

"We've been back some months," Rosie explained. "We've been living here in the town with a boy called Esram and... and Carrik, too. Carrik is changed! What happened to him?"

"You've met Esram?" Morwen lost some of her calm. "How is he? Does he speak of me?"

A satisfied smirk passed over Rosie's face. So Luke did have a rival for the lovely Morwen? Forgetting all about sisterly love, Rosie made things very plain.

"Oh yes, he often talks about you. He never stops, actually. Even in prison."

Morwen seemed dismayed. "In prison? Esram is in prison?"

"Oh yes, and Carrik too. Didn't he –," she pointed to Lord Veritan, "Didn't he tell you anything?"

"Only that he wanted us to go with him, he had a surprise for us," Petroc answered. "We met him in the Dark Forest and he had brought that horse for us and said we were to trust him, so we did. Why are Carrik and Esram in prison? How can they tell people about Salvis in prison?"

"They can tell people just what they need to hear," Luke grinned. "Sit down and we'll explain."

So Luke told them about Reuben and Holly and about how Carrik had been falsely accused and how the Children of the Second Morning had given their hearts to Salvis and about how he and Rosie were helping the children to learn more about the King.

In his turn, Petroc told them how they had rebuilt his father's farm, and that his mother was now back home. He also told them that they could trust Esram and Carrik completely. Esram had once saved Petroc's life by pulling him from the sea and he had also rescued Morwen from Bellum's castle.

It was a wonderful time for them all.

Too soon, Lord Veritan called. Petroc and Morwen stood up.

"We have to go," Petroc sighed. "Luke, Rosie, we have to go home now." He sounded very sad.

"I want to go with you," said Rosie. "I hate it in the town. I want to go back to your farm."

"You cannot," Morwen told her, speaking ever so gently. "The King must have brought you here for a purpose. You must continue to help the children of the town."

They all hugged each other. Then, as quickly as they had arrived, Petroc and Morwen were gone, riding back to their own part of the island with Lord Veritan acting as their protector and guide.

Veritan had not even spoken to Luke and Rosie, yet his being there reassured them that the King was aware of their unhappiness and was watching over them.

Once again Luke and Rosie were alone but now they were no longer lonely.

Chapter 16

Guardian Law

As they watched their friends ride away with Lord Veritan, a happiness came into their hearts, a feeling of contentment and well-being that neither Luke nor Rosie had known when they set out that day.

"I feel better now," said Rosie.

"So do I. It's like we have this special job to do for the King and now we're sure what it is. It makes sense of why we've come here."

Luke knew that there was another, unspoken reason he'd returned to Karensa. He knew that Salvis was calling him home, drawing him back with his gentle love. Luke had been sure of this from the moment he had set eyes on Petroc and Morwen. Being with them had reminded him of how wonderful it was to serve the King.

"We have to help the Children of the Second Morning," Rosie agreed. "Oh, but I still want to see Salvis so much."

"So do I," he replied.

Rosie sighed. "I suppose we'd better go."

They took a last look in the direction of the Royal Palace. It was not there! The Palace had disappeared! So had Bellum's castle and the Dark Forest.

"Oh no!" Rosie exclaimed. "The mist has come down. What shall we do?"

"Reuben said we should go back to the town if the mist came down. That's what we must do."

"But where is the town? Which way?"

Luke scratched his head. He was trying not to panic, but with the mist swirling all around them, covering everything, it was hard not to be afraid. They could just about see each other, and that was all. It had come down so quickly. One minute the sun had been shining and the next, damp, swirling fronds of white were everywhere.

"It reminds me of the day the dolphins first brought us here," Rosie whispered.

Luke shivered. He didn't want to be reminded of that day when he had very nearly drowned.

"Well, we have to go down the hill," he said, "because we climbed up the hill to get here. If we go down, we should come back to the path and maybe we'll recognise some of the rocks."

Rosie didn't answer. All the granite boulders looked the same. They were big, grey and round!

They had to do something. They couldn't stay here and wait for the mist to clear. It might take all night and they were already cold and wet. No matter how they huddled into their cloaks, the woollen material did nothing to prevent the damp from soaking through to their skins. They began to feel very, very miserable.

Soon, as well as feeling wretched, they were forced to admit that they had completely lost their way.

"I'm scared," Rosie said, shivering.

"So am I," Luke admitted.

"I've got an idea. If we keep turning left, we must come somewhere soon, either the town, or a farm, or even the sea."

Luke didn't have a better idea, so that was what they did, but as they didn't know this part of the island very well, they stood no chance of finding their way through the mist. It was not long before they knew that they were lost.

"Luke, what shall we do?" Rosie said again.

Her brother was about to tell her, very forcefully, that he didn't know, when a dark shape moved silently towards them. The shape appeared to have wings which flapped as the creature moved. Luke and Rosie felt the hairs on the back of their necks prickle.

"A ghost!" Rosie muttered, feeling sick and clutching hold of Luke's arm.

"There are no such things!" he replied, in a way that was totally unconvincing.

As they froze in fear, their scalps tingling, the shape called their names.

"Luke, Rosie, I have searched everywhere for you!"

"Jay!" Rosie squealed. "Luke, it's only Jay! We shall be safe now! He'll know the way home!"

It was indeed their friend, Jay. The flapping had been his loose cloak.

"I am so thankful to find you!" Jay panted, obviously very out of breath. "Where have you been? Something so terrible is happening! It is Carrik and Esram! They are in danger!"

Luke tried to imagine what his dad would say in this situation. Dad was pretty good in a crisis. He thought he knew. "You must calm down and get your breath back, then tell us what's happened."

Jay bent forward, his hands on his knees, and

after a minute his breathing was easier.

"Can you speak now?" asked Luke.

"Well enough," Jay straightened up. His face was red and sweaty and streaked with dirt. "My brother, Hawk, is one of the Guardians. I heard him talking to my father. There are plans being made by the Guardians to be rid of Carrik and Esram for ever."

"But they can't do that!" Rosie spluttered. "They can't break their own law."

"No, but there are always ways around laws. Tomas has discovered that when the people visit Carrik in prison, he is talking to them about Salvis and he is encouraging them to give their loyalty to the King. Tomas cannot stop the visits, because they are now Guardian Law, so he is setting Carrik and Esram free."

"That must be good?" Rosie asked, confused.

"No, not good, Rosie. Very bad. They are to be put into a boat and released from the Bay of Perils at sunset tonight."

"In the dark?" Luke cried. "They won't see the rocks!"

"It is not only the dark and the rocks, Luke. The Bay of Perils is the most dangerous place on the whole of Karensa. Even on a calm day, the seas are rough there. At high tide tonight, the waves will be as big as houses. The boat will be sure to capsize. They must both be drowned. They cannot survive such a journey. And what they are doing is quite lawful. They are not actually killing anyone, are they? That really would break their own law for their law does not execute prisoners. They are only saying that Carrik's prison term is over and so they

113

are setting them both free."

"What shall we do?" said Luke, trying to get his head around this and thinking that a law that could be used in such a way was no law at all.

"I am calling a meeting of the Children of the Second Morning," Jay told him. "We must get together and decide what is the best thing to do. We cannot stand by and let this happen, but we shall all be punished by our parents when they find out that we have disobeyed them and given our hearts to the King. I have found some of the children and they are already on their way to the meeting place, but I have not found others, and we must have everyone there for this meeting. I could not find Holly or Lindis. You must find them for me. They are most likely together –"

"They usually are," Rosie interrupted bitterly.

Jay ignored the interruption. "We must all meet. We must all decide what to do. It cannot be my decision alone. All the children have something to lose when it is discovered that we belong to the King."

"We cannot let that stop us!" Luke cried, thinking of how Esram had once pulled Petroc from the sea. Rosie echoed him.

"Of course not," Jay agreed. "But we must move quickly or we shall be too late."

Even as he spoke, the mist lifted, and Luke and Rosie found that they had been on the right path all the time, for the town was in front of them, the sea sparkling in the sunlight.

Chapter 17

"Children prepared to fight"

Holly and Lindis were sitting on the white stone wall in the yard behind the shop when Luke and Rosie raced up to them. They ran through the shop so quickly that Luke knocked down three pairs of boots, and in spite of Reuben's protest he didn't stop to pick them up.

The two girls wore colourful new tunics which were cool enough for the Time of New Birth. Holly was dressed in lilac and Lindis in a dark, russet colour which suited her olive skin and made her eyes look even bigger and darker. Holly had discovered beads and bracelets in the attic and they had spent the afternoon dressing each other's hair with bright ribbons and combs. They had also found a bottle of perfume and used quite a lot of it on themselves.

When Rosie raced up to her, Holly wrinkled her nose in disgust. "Rosie, how could you be so smelly? You should go inside and have a wash."

"Yes, you should," Lindis giggled, holding her nose. "You are a smelly child!"

"So would you be if you moved yourself!" Rosie retorted, trying to smell underneath her arms without their seeing. There was no such thing as deodorant on Karensa and she was hot and stressed.

115

"Never mind all that," Luke interrupted. "Where have you been? Jay has been looking for you! This is an emergency! There's to be a meeting of the Children of the Second Morning and you have to come. Both of you! Now!"

Holly yawned lazily. "Yes, we did hear Jay, but we were busy and chose not to answer him. Actually, I do not have to do anything or go anywhere that I do not want to do, boy!"

"Oh, yes you do, Holly!" Luke replied. "This is serious. This time you must come. Carrik and Esram are in danger! They are going to be set adrift in a boat from the Bay of Perils. If we don't help them, they will drown."

"Oh do not be so dramatic, boy!" Holly laughed. She was obviously showing off in front of Lindis now that Luke and Rosie were servants in the household. "Another thing, I think you should call me 'Miss Holly' from now on. That is what my father's servants should call me, I believe."

Luke glared at her, determined that he was not going to call her any such thing. Beneath the stare of his grey eyes, Holly looked away.

"Anyway, I am not coming," she muttered.

Rosie and Luke exchanged glances.

"She has to come!" Rosie cried. "Jay said no-one must be left out!"

"You cannot make her," Lindis pointed out.

"You persuade her, then," said Rosie, desperately.

Lindis smiled in a lazy sort of way. "Me? Why should I? She may please herself what she does. However, I shall come... Holly, shall you change your mind?"

Holly shook her head stubbornly. Lindis shrugged and linked arms with a reluctant Rosie, who was not at all happy that they had even told Lindis what was going on. She did not trust her, but Jay had said to ask everyone, and that included Lindis.

"It is just me then, Rosie," Lindis whispered. "But you do not want me, do you? You know I will never be your friend? Oh, and Rosie... You do need a wash."

After they had gone, Reuben came out into the yard. He was rubbing his head in a vague sort of way.

"What was that about Carrik?" he asked. "Where has he gone? I sent him out to look for the children a while ago and he has not yet returned."

Holly stared at him in disbelief. He must be talking about the day he was attacked. Some of his memory had returned. It seemed that Carrik had been telling the truth all the time.

The Children of the Second Morning sat in a semicircle in the barn while Jay told them what was going on. When he had finished, he asked them what action they should take.

"We have to stop them," said one small boy. "We cannot let Esram die! I like Esram!"

"So do I! We must help them!"

Lindis protested. "The Guardians cannot be doing anything wrong. Their law is just and fair and they will not break that law. They will not hurt Carrik and Esram. My father, Tomas, would not allow it."

No-one took any notice of her and when she realised that she was being ignored, she blushed deeply and set her soft, full mouth in a hard line.

Luke spoke up. "I believe we have to save them," he said. "We cannot let them be drowned. We should go down to the Bay of Perils, or whatever it's called, and tell the Guardians that we are loyal to the King and do not want their law."

"Many of us will be in trouble," Jay pointed out. "My brother is one of the Guardians and my father is friendly with them. I know I shall be punished when they find out what I have done, yet I will risk this for Esram. He was always true to the Children of the Second Morning. He was the first to tell us about the King, then he brought Luke and Rosie to us to finish the telling and to show us how we can belong to the King once more."

"I know I shall be in trouble," one of the older girls groaned. "We have to help them, though. We cannot let this thing be done to them."

"No, we cannot simply do nothing!"

"We should do as Luke said!"

"No, there must be another way!"

In the discussion that followed, no-one noticed Lindis slip away, pulling down the iron bar on the door behind her so that they were locked inside.

"That is decided then," said Jay when they had reached an agreement. "We shall go now to the Bay of Perils and try to stop them. All in favour raise their hands!"

Every hand went up and this was followed by a loud cheer.

"The Children of the Second Morning are prepared to fight for what they believe!" Jay shouted, and went to the door. "It's bolted!" he cried in disbelief. "We are locked in!"

Rosie looked around the barn. "Lindis has gone," she said. "It must have been her. Oh, I knew we shouldn't have told her anything about this! I told you not to trust her, Luke!"

"It can't be locked," Luke muttered, then after bruising his hand trying to open it, he found that it was.

What could they do? Luke and Jay and one or two of the older boys tried to break it down but the door was heavy and bound with iron. It refused to move.

Rosie remembered another time when she and Luke had been made prisoners, the night Salvis died. That time, Morwen had set them free. Rosie looked at her brother and he gave her a funny sort of smile. He remembered, too.

"There is nothing we can do to escape!" Jay cried. "All this has been for nothing!"

To make herself feel better and to lift their spirits, Rosie began to sing.

"The Children of the Second Morning,
Awaiting the New Day's dawning.
Children against the night,
Seeking the Spirit's light..."

Her voice tailed away as no-one joined in.

Then, very softly, from the other side of the door, came a faint response.

"Children prepared to fight,
Standing for truth and right..."

Rosie gasped. "Holly! Is that you?" Then they both finished the song together, with the other children joining in.

"We're the Children of the Second Morning,
Hearts ready for the New Day's dawning."

As the last notes of the song ended, another big cheer went up, and when Holly lifted the iron bolt and opened the door, there was yet another cheer.

Holly threw her arms around Rosie. "I'm so sorry, Rosie, I was wrong. I know Carrik did not do those things to my father. Please forgive me, both of you. And... and you do not really smell."

Rosie grinned. "I do, but I don't care. Of course we forgive you, Holly. We're glad you're back with us. How did you know what had happened?"

"I met Lindis on the way here. She told me what she had done. I do not like her any more, I think."

"Where is she now?" Rosie asked, curious and more than a little suspicious, not of Holly but of Lindis.

"Ah well, you may ask," Holly grinned. "I met her on the corner of the farm, by the pig pen, and she fell in."

"Fell?" Jay asked sternly.

"Sort of fell in. I dare say she has gone home for a bath."

Rosie burst out laughing, but her brother and Jay were getting impatient.

"The sun will soon be setting," Jay told them. "The tide will turn within the half hour, so if we are to save Carrik and Esram, we must go now, or I fear it will be too late."

Chapter 18

We serve the King

The way from Jay's barn to the Bay of Perils had never seemed so far. The two biggest boys carried the smallest children on their shoulders. Even so, by the time they all arrived at the bay, the sun was setting, a pale pink globe fading into the mist surrounding the island.

A crowd had gathered on the rocky shore that formed a natural harbour. Several Guardians had assembled at the narrow pier from where Luke and Esram had once rescued the sea gulls from the torn fishing nets.

Rosie groaned. "Oh no! They've already put Carrik and Esram into the boat!"

"The tide is ready to turn!" cried Jay.

The arrival of the children caused a stir in the crowd as parents called angrily to them to keep out of danger. They were ignored. They were not even heard.

The children stood at the place where the path joined the pier. Even in the shelter of the bay, the sea was already wild, the highest waves crashing up to the pier.

The small rowing boat, moored to the pier, was rocking crazily and Carrik and Esram sat one at each end of the boat, clinging desperately to the sides. There were no oars.

Carrik seemed calm. Esram looked calm, but his face was very white.

Indignation rose in the pit of Luke's stomach.

"This is not fair!" he cried. "Look, they've put chains on their feet! They can't possibly survive now! If they fall into the water, they won't be able to swim with their feet chained up. If this is your law here, it's no law at all and I don't think much of it!"

Tomas, standing on the pier, shouted angrily.

"Tell those children to go back or they shall go into the sea with their friends!"

Scared parents called frantically to their sons and daughters, but in vain. Led by Holly, the children walked in single file down to the jetty.

Holly walked right along to where the boat was moored and stood in front of it with her back to the sea. Her face was scared but determined, her chin jutting out in a familiar gesture of defiance. Holly knew exactly what she was going to do and why she was doing it.

"I am Holly," she said in a loud voice. "I am a Child of the Second Morning. Salvis is my Lord and I will serve him and the King for ever. Before you cut the boat free, you must move me."

With those words, she stood on the very edge of the pier, her back to the sea. In such a position, her heels already over the edge of the pier, she would be sure to lose her balance and fall backwards into the water if anyone touched her.

Without hesitation, Jay followed her and repeated her words, then he stood by her side.

"I am Jay. I am a Child of the Second Morning and Salvis is my Lord..."

He was followed by a little girl who could not have been more than six or seven years old.

"I am Temi. I am a Child of the Second Morning..."

"I am Robin..."

"I am Brinn..."

One by one, each of the children pledged their loyalty to Salvis as they stood holding hands in a line along the narrow pier, each willing to put their own lives in danger to save Esram, who they had made their friend.

Luke alone hesitated. If he made a decision now, it must be a decision for the rest of his life. He knew that this time he would not turn away from Salvis no matter how he felt or what happened. This time he would stay loyal, whether on Karensa or back home in Poldawn.

He looked at the two figures in the small boat. Once he had hated Carrik for the way he had treated Petroc and his family, but Petroc and Morwen had both forgiven him. If they forgave Carrik, then so must he. He looked again at this middle-aged man who now loved the King so much he was willing to give up his freedom and even to die for him. He looked at Esram who had saved Petroc's life and rescued Morwen from Bellum's castle.

Luke walked slowly along the pier. The cobbles were slippy and covered in seaweed, and salt spray was in his face so that he couldn't see clearly where he was going, but he walked to the very end of the pier, where dark waves were crashing right over the stones. His voice was firm and resolute.

"I am Luke. I am a Child of the Second Morning. Salvis is my Lord and will always be my Lord, and

I ask him to forgive me for turning away from him. I come back to him now and I will serve the King for ever in any way he asks me to. Before you cut the boat free, you must first move me."

Then he, too, stood in the line. The children did not falter. As the swell of the sea grew higher, spray washed right over them and the power of each wave threatened to pull them into the sea.

Luke stole a glance over his shoulder to the boat and knew that he had done the right thing. Carrik's face was buried in his hands but Esram's hands were raised in praise to the King.

The Children of the Second Morning had chosen the way they would fight.

As they stood there, each of them so scared, yet each of them trusting the King to help them, Lindis arrived.

Scrubbed clean and in fresh clothes, she ran to Tomas.

"Father! These children have betrayed the Guardians! They have been meeting in secret in Jay's barn. They deserve to be punished!" She pointed to Rosie. "It was her – she was the one to blame!" she added spitefully.

Tomas looked even more angry, if that was possible. He called his men to his side.

"The Guardians will not tolerate disobedience! Cast these traitors into the sea! If they stand in such a ridiculous position, they must expect to get hurt! If you children move now, I will allow your parents to punish you as you deserve. If you do not move, we will move you and you must drown!"

The children did not move. Rosie was visibly

shaking.

"Salvis, Salvis, Salvis," was all she could think of to say and she repeated it over and over again.

A few of the Guardians moved to obey Tomas, but then they hesitated, unwilling to carry out such a harsh command.

One of them, it must have been Hawk, said, "Sir, these are only children. One is my young brother, Jay. You cannot mean us to do this?"

"We cannot hurt children," another Guardian added. "There is my son, and my little daughter, only six years old. I... I have always obeyed you, sir, but I cannot do so now."

"Then I shall carry out the order myself," Tomas roared in a voice that did not sound very different from Bellum's voice.

Tomas moved towards Luke, who was the most vulnerable. Luke closed his eyes and, just like Rosie, could only repeat the name of Salvis as he waited for the black waters to close over him. All he could think of was that he would not see Dad or Stacey again. He hoped someone would look after Pepper.

Yet before Tomas could reach him, they were deafened by the noise of a hundred screaming gulls and the line of children was surrounded by sea birds!

The gulls flew all about them, white feathers everywhere, black button eyes glinting, and all of them squalling loudly, making it impossible for Tomas to reach them. No-one could touch them.

Holly laughed out loud above the noise the gulls were making. "It is the birds we helped to get free from the fishing nets! They have not forgotten us!

They are repaying our kindness!"

"So they are!" Luke laughed too, at a time when he did not feel at all like laughing. He remembered that on Karensa there was a special understanding between man and the animal kingdom. Jay laughed, even though he did not understand what they were laughing about.

Rosie continued to whisper, "Salvis, Salvis, Salvis..."

As the sea birds circled around them, Tomas and Lindis stood and watched helplessly, growing more and more angry, especially as the gulls covered them both in droppings so that Tomas' yellow hair turned white. Lindis need not have bothered to wash away the mud from the pig pen.

In the middle of all the confusion, Reuben arrived.

Reuben seemed very agitated. He trotted down to the pier as fast as his short legs and his rounded stomach would allow.

"You must not do this, my friends! No, no, this man was not to blame for what happened to me! It was not him! I remember now! It was not Carrik!" He pointed to Tomas. "It was two of his Guardians, and I did not see their faces because they wore helmets with visors. Carrik had left the house to find the children for me!"

"What of the clasp?" one of the Guardians called.

"Carrik told me he had lost the clasp that morning. No, no, you must set Carrik and the boy free!"

Even as he spoke, the gulls flew away. Tomas, knowing that he had lost the battle, took his daughter's arm and dragged her off towards the town. Tomas had been defeated by a group of children and a flock of sea gulls and an old man.

Luke and Rosie knew that really, he had been defeated by the King's own power, for the King was looking after them. Maybe the King had healed Reuben's memory at just the right moment in time? He might have done.

The children stood on the slippery pier and Holly led them in a mighty cheer. This time the crowd joined in as, with Reuben, they surged forwards to haul Carrik and Esram to safety.

Chapter 19

"The battle belongs to the Lord"

The crowd rushed towards them and Carrik was concerned that the very children who had saved their lives would be pushed into the sea as the sudden mass of people converged on the narrow stone pier.

"Children! Move back to the shore so that others have room to pass you!" Carrik shouted, but no-one heard him.

"Uncle," Esram sighed. "I cannot believe we are safe at last. I had thought to die today."

"Yet you did not once cry out," Carrik told him. "Esram, you were very brave. I was proud of you. Real bravery is not giving in to your fears."

Esram had not felt brave. Earlier in the day, when four Guardians had come to their cell and told them they were to be released, Esram's heart had leapt with joy, for he had been watching the coming of the Time of New Birth from the window, and longed to be out on the moors or in the fields where the hedgerows were bright with new leaves.

He longed to walk freely by the sea shore and climb over the rocks and breathe in the fresh, salty air.

When the four Guardians marched them down to the Bay of Perils, their suspicions were aroused.

"We cannot set sail from here," Carrik objected

when they saw the boat waiting.

One of the Guardians laughed harshly. "We said you were to be set free. We did not say how this was to be done, did we? Free is free. There is no law that says you have to be released in any special way. You have served your term in prison. Now you are free!" He laughed again.

Esram looked at Carrik, who in turn gave his nephew's shoulder a reassuring squeeze.

"Are we... are we to go in the boat?" Esram asked.

The youngest of the Guardians nodded. He could not look Esram in the eye.

The boat was moored to an iron ladder which was built into the wall of the pier, and Esram and Carrik were told to climb down. There was no sense in arguing because if they showed any resistance, they were likely to fall into the heaving sea.

As they sat one each end of the small wooden craft, Esram looked down at the angry water, the swell now black in the light from the setting sun. Esram was a very strong swimmer. He might stand a chance, if they didn't run into rocks in the dark.

When chains were put on their ankles, he knew that they stood no chance at all.

"Why are you doing this?" Carrik cried.

"It is only what you deserve! Coming here, telling lies about Salvis –"

"They are not lies!" Carrik protested.

"Lies! They are lies! You wrecked poor Reuben's shop, too!"

"I did not," Carrik reasoned with them. "As for the boy, he has done nothing. At least let him go free."

"You shall both go free," he was told.

"So it seems," Carrik replied, pointing to the chains.

The Guardians laughed. "There is no law against that!"

Carrik did not say any more. He knew that it was not Carrik and Esram that these men were afraid of, it was the King.

They had sensed the King's power in each of them and wanted to be rid of them.

The younger Guardian locked the chain around Esram's ankles.

"I... I am sorry, boy. I only obey orders. I wish it could be another way..."

Esram looked away. It was clear they were to die and he was relieved that Carrik did not try to hide it from him.

"By tonight we shall both be in the Royal Palace with Salvis. There we shall live for ever," he whispered.

Esram did not want to be in the Royal Palace. He wanted to be back on Petroc's farm with Morwen. The weeks he had spent there had been the only truly happy time of his life. He was fourteen years old. He didn't want to die.

Even as he struggled to stop his teeth from chattering with fear, he knew that they were not on their own. Salvis was with them. He knew everything that was happening to them. They couldn't see him but they knew that he was there and their fears began to subside into a sort of acceptance, almost a peace.

It was then that the children arrived...

* * *

Luke and Jay climbed down the iron ladder into the boat. Luke had the keys and was unlocking their chains.

When Esram stood up, his legs gave way and he sat down again so suddenly that the boat almost overturned.

Luke caught him. "Ho there, Esram, get up more slowly next time! You don't want to fall in the sea now or we've wasted our time rescuing you!"

Esram laughed, but the next time, he took Luke's advice and he was able to climb up the ladder to the pier. Carrik went last, following behind the boys.

They were greeted as heroes by the crowd, who cheered and shouted and jumped up and down, freeing themselves at last from the control of the Guardians, at least for a little while.

It was Rosie who saw the wave approaching. She screamed.

"Look! A tidal wave! Run!"

It wasn't exactly a tidal wave but it was high enough. They raced to the safety of the shore just as the wave broke with a mighty crash over the stone jetty.

In seconds, the rowing boat disappeared, splintered by the power of the ocean.

Luke sat down suddenly. "That was close!" he said.

As the sun faded, Carrik stood on the highest rock. The people sat round him, and he explained again about how much the King loved them and why he had sent his son, Salvis, to die for them.

This time, they listened. This time, Reuben pledged his loyalty to Salvis. This time, others followed him. This time, the Children of the Second Morning were able to lead their own parents into the King's service as Carrik spoke to them all and helped them.

It was a sweet moment and one never to be forgotten in the history of Karensa.

"The battle belongs to the Lord," said Luke. "There is nothing more we need do here."

Rosie slipped her hand into his. "It must be time now for us to go home?" she whispered.

"Are you ready to go?"

"I... I think so. I should have liked to know Holly better, and Esram, too, but they don't really need us. We have seen Petroc and Morwen. I believe it's time for us to go home."

"I feel we should go to the barn."

"Why?"

"I don't know. I just do. Ask Holly and Esram if they want to come."

Holly and Esram agreed, so for the last time they set off together to the secret meeting place of the Children of the Second Morning, leaving Carrik and the other children to continue the King's work.

A little way off, on the edge of the town, a dark-haired man sat on a black horse. Lord Bellum had heard what had happened and was waiting for Tomas and Lindis to arrive. His face was more angry than ever before.

When Tomas and Lindis saw him, they both fell to the ground in fear of their lives.

"You failed!" Bellum's voice sounded like an angry serpent waiting to strike. "Tomas, you failed me after all."

Bellum leapt from his horse and hauled Lindis to her feet. She screamed as her breath was forced from her body.

"You stupid child!" he hissed. "Where are your fine looks now? What are you? No longer a nut-brown maid! A silly child covered in bird droppings! I had thought you were my servant! I gave you my power! What have you done with it?"

"I am your servant, master!" Lindis whined.

"My servants do not fail me. And they do not degrade themselves by walking the streets of the town covered in bird droppings! To fail me is deserving of death!"

He threw Lindis so that she landed face down in the muddy gutter.

"That is the place for those who fail!" he cried. "You are even dirtier now, and it suits you well!"

Tomas, fearful for their safety, was thinking fast. He crawled towards Lord Bellum and worshipped him in the way the dark-haired lord loved. Bellum never could resist worship. He craved it more than wealth, more than power. The desire for worship had made him disobey the King and so be cast from the Royal Palace.

"Great master, we have not failed," said Tomas, his thoughts racing as though his life depended on them, which it probably did. "Only one battle has been lost. We have other plans. Plans that will please you. Wait and see what happens when food is kept from the people who follow the King. Wait until they have no dinner to give their children and then see whom they serve..."

Bellum crossed over to Lindis and pulled her to

her feet and, as she stood crying and trembling before him, he roughly snatched the gold chain from her neck.

"This reward has not been earned." He stared at Lindis in a way that caused her to be ashamed of her appearance. Suddenly his voice deepened and he spoke softly. "Yet, even so, Lindis, I see my power in your eyes. Are you still willing to serve me?"

"Yes, master. You know I am willing."

"Then I will hear these plans. Yes, I will hear them."

So the struggle continued...

Holly lit the candles in the barn and the four of them sat quietly, not needing words to express their friendship.

"We shall have no use for this place any more," Holly sighed, a little sadly. "We have no secrets now. My father has pledged his loyalty to Lord Salvis; so have the other children's parents. Just like me."

"Just like you, Holly," a soft voice agreed.

He stood by the door, tall and slim and dressed simply in a grey tunic belted with leather and a blue woollen cloak. Holly knew at once who he was, even though she had never seen him before.

"Lord Salvis," she breathed, and fell to her knees.

The other children followed. Kneeling at his feet seemed the natural place to be. It was the place they wanted to be.

Rosie gazed up at the King's son and all her longing was met in his kind eyes. She began to speak, but Salvis put a finger to his lips to silence her.

Then he smiled at her as if they both shared a great secret.

As they knelt there quietly, Esram learnt all he needed to know to tell others about Salvis, for now he had seen him for himself and felt the awesomeness of his presence.

Holly at last knew that she was loved just as she was, not as she would like to be, and in this knowledge found a new confidence.

Rosie could have stayed there for ever.

Cold flames of love and peace washed over them and time stood still as the children forgot everything except Salvis, and he blessed them, just by being with them.

Chapter 20

"Safe in his hands"

They sat at his feet and Salvis had a special word for each of them, but when it was Luke's turn, the King's son took his hands, holding them together and covering them with his own.

"How do you feel now, Luke?" he asked.

"Safe... like... like I never want to move away."

"This is how I care about you. When you first said you were sorry and asked me into your life, I promised never to leave you. Now take away your hands."

Luke did as Salvis asked, but before he could put his hands down, Salvis caught them again and held them more tightly than before. This time Luke could not pull his hands away.

"You see, even when you turn away from me, I will seek you and call you back again. I will never let you go."

With that wonderful promise ringing in his ears, Luke forgot all about the others and what they might think of him. The only thing that mattered was Salvis and the touch of his hands, holding him safely.

"Why did you leave me, Luke?" Salvis asked, sadly.

Luke tried to be honest. "I... I don't know, Lord. I did try to tell some of my friends who you really are, but they laughed and then... then..."

"Then you were not prepared to lose your friends so you walked with them, even though you knew it was wrong for you?"

Luke nodded miserably.

"Were you happy walking with them?" asked Salvis gently.

"No, not really... Salvis, that was you in the park on Christmas Eve, wasn't it?"

"Oh yes, Luke, it was me. You knew that when you asked me who I really was, just like you did in the cave. You knew the answer well enough, but you closed your eyes to the truth."

Luke hung his head, ashamed. "So you brought me here?"

"Are you sorry I did?"

Luke hesitated. He hadn't liked the far side of the island. He would sooner have stayed with his friends, Petroc and Morwen, but he remembered the night the Children of the Second Morning had turned to the King, here, in this very barn. Afterwards they had all praised the King like never before. He thought of how he had been aware of Salvis the minute he had set foot on Karensa. He thought of how great it had been, seeing Petroc and Morwen only that very morning.

"Lord, did you bring Petroc and Morwen to us today?"

"Oh Luke," Salvis sighed. "Don't you realise that I will supply all your needs? I knew that you both needed to see your friends before you even knew it yourselves."

"Then... will we be seeing them again?"

Salvis did not reply. His only answer was a gentle

smile. "Remember this, Luke," Salvis told him, "I am always with you. Even when you cannot see me, I am there. Even when you cannot feel my presence, I am there. I will always live in your heart, just as I promised. Now it is time for you to return home to Poldawn. There you must tell your friends about me. Some may not be your friends any more when you do tell them. Some may laugh. Do not let that stop you. It is me they laugh at, not you, so do not be hurt by their laughter. Anything they do to you, they did to me first."

Luke nodded, not liking all he heard, but knowing it was the truth. Following the King was not an easy life, but it was the best life ever.

"One thing more, Luke," Salvis went on. "Will you always stay loyal?"

"Yes... yes I will this time, Lord."

"Even though you may lose some of your friends?"

"Yes, Lord, you know I will."

"Do you really mean that, with all your heart?"

Luke sighed. "Lord, you know I mean it. Why do you keep asking me? You've asked me three times!"

"Yes," Salvis whispered, so quietly that only Luke could hear. "Yes, I have asked you three times, Luke, just as you denied me three times in Bellum's castle on the night I died. Now be healed of the guilt you carry. I have forgiven you. Forgive yourself."

Luke stared at Salvis, too shocked to reply. It was true, he had never forgiven himself for running away.

A stream of healing power flowed through him,

cleansing him of the hurt he felt deep inside. Just as Rosie had cried because she longed to see Salvis, now Luke shed his own tears, and it did not seem to matter that he was too old to cry. Afterwards, the pain was washed away for evermore.

"Now," said Salvis, "you really are ready to tell your friends that which they need to hear." In a much louder voice he added, "Luke, Rosie, it is time to go home."

They got up, each of them stunned by what was happening, but each of them changed in some way since they had met Salvis.

Luke and Esram looked at each other, both feeling suddenly awkward.

Esram said, "I thought I would die this day."

"So did I," Luke agreed, and shuddered at the memory of the dark, heaving water.

They had only known each other for a short while. Much of that time, Esram had spent in prison, but they both had the King's power and that power made them brothers.

Holly slipped her hand through Rosie's arm. "I don't need to be like anyone else. I know the King loves me, just as I am. Oh, I shall miss you, Rosie. You never did my hair like you said you would."

"Things happened to stop me," Rosie said wryly. "Maybe next time? We shall be back, one day."

Salvis did not deny it. The four young people hugged each other, then Esram and Holly were gone, leaving quickly.

All of a sudden, Salvis threw back his head and laughed, resting an arm on each of their shoulders. It was a wonderful laugh and Karensa laughed with him, from the eagles soaring over the high moors to the smallest field mouse. The joy of Salvis was the joy of creation.

"Oh Luke, it is so good to have you back with me!"

"It's good to be back, Lord," Luke answered, then he and Rosie joined in the laughter. They couldn't help it. All three laughed until they felt their sides would burst.

At last it was over. Salvis showed them a wooden door in the barn that they had never noticed before, just as they had never seen the door in the chapel wall at Poldawn. Salvis pushed the door and it swung open.

"There's nothing there! Everywhere's dark!" Rosie cried in dismay, turning round to Salvis.

Salvis had gone. They were alone.

"I believe we have to go through the door," said Luke.

"We can't! There might be nothing there! We could fall into nothing, like a black hole in space!"

"We have to take a step of faith and trust Salvis to be with us," her brother replied.

"I don't dare!"

"Yes, Rosie," said Luke, "you do dare." He felt very strong, knowing this was how Salvis wanted them to live from now on, trusting him to be there. "Hold my hand, Rosie. Trust Salvis and trust me."

Rosie slipped her hand into his and thought of all the wonderful things Salvis had just said to her, things she would never share.

"Yes," she said, "I do dare."

So they went through the door together and stepped out into the darkness.

* * *

Rosie's Bible was still where she had left it, on a chair in the small chapel. It was very quiet. Soon someone would switch off the lights and lock the door.

They didn't leave right away, but sat for a while.

"We're home," Rosie whispered. "We didn't stay there as long as last time."

"We stayed as long as we needed. I feel... I feel so..." Luke could never find the words to express the peace he felt in his heart. Better than before. Better than the first time they had come home. Then they had not really understood who Salvis was.

Luke took Rosie's Bible from her and flicked through it until he found the page he was looking for, near the very end, in the book of Hebrews. He found Chapter Thirteen.

"Here it is! Listen to this, Rosie. *'God said, I will never leave you or forsake you.'* That's what Salvis said to me."

Rosie moved her finger down the page. "Listen to this, then. *'Jesus is the same yesterday, today and forever.'* When we came home before, we knew that we should tell our friends about Jesus, but we didn't do that really, did we? Jesus died for us all so that we can be forgiven for everything we've done wrong."

They thought about this for a while.

"D'you remember last time we went home from Karensa?" Rosie went on. "We found Mum's Bible and stayed up all night, reading it and looking at the stars and thinking about the island... It's different this time, isn't it?"

"Yes, it is. I feel more... more... This time I just

feel everything is right with us."

He wasn't explaining himself very well, but his sister seemed to understand.

Luke closed the Bible and just as they were about to leave, they thought they glimpsed a tall, slim figure dressed in grey, then he was gone.

Luke and Rosie laughed again. They had left Karensa behind, but such a great King could not be confined to one small island, or even one small planet. He was everywhere. He was still with them and would be with them until the end of time.

The story of the Great King and his Son will be told every day of every week of every month of every year until the whole world has heard it.

Luke was determined that he was going to tell his own friends about Jesus, and he knew that the Great King would be with him to help him as he stepped out in faith and obedience.

Rosie held her Bible close to her heart. "The Great King has promised never to leave us or forsake us. We shall always be safe in his hands."

THE BEGINNING
OF THE END

Look out for the final book in the Tales of Karensa *series...*

Silver Serpent, Golden Sword
Jean Cullop

"This is the golden sword of truth, which can never be defeated in battle," said Lord Veritan. "The coming times will be very hard for the King's people. I am here to prepare you for battle. Lord Bellum and the Guardians have taken the silver serpent as their emblem, but that serpent will never overcome the golden sword. Now, you must all kneel."

No-one spoke. The young people sensed that something very special was about to happen.

They knelt in this place that meant so much to Luke and Petroc, and the woodland became strangely silent. No creature stirred. It was as though the Dark Forest sensed the awesome nearness of its Creator.

"I do this with the King's authority," Veritan told them in a very serious voice. "You must keep perfectly still. I am going to anoint each one of you with the sword of truth."

He passed the mighty sword over their heads, so close that its two-edged blade touched their hair. As the sword moved, the light of day deepened to that of a glorious sunset.

When it was done, and daylight returned, Veritan spoke even more seriously. "The truth of the King's word will be your protection. Some of you will be called to suffer for your loyalty to the King..."

ISBN 1 85999 555 1

The earlier books in the Tales of Karensa *series...*

Where Dolphins race with Rainbows
Jean Cullop

"Welcome to Karensa."
Luke opened his eyes, blinking against the strong sunlight. He was sprawled on his back on soft, dry sand. In front of him the sea was calm and deepest blue, the waves lapping gently against the shore.

So the mist and the storm were a dream? He was safely back at Poldawn.

But as he struggled to sit up he realised that there had been no dream. This was not Poldawn. This was a bay of clean, flat sand surrounded by cliffs, lush with flowering plants and bushes unlike anything he had ever imagined. What was more, he was being watched by a group of the strangest looking people he had ever seen.

ISBN 1 85999 383 4

Castle of Shadows
Jean Cullop

The King gave a loud cry, a cry that resounded through the entire universe. "Now my Son who was dead is alive again! Now my people can come to me once more! Now, Salvis, you wear your royal robes... One day you will judge the people of Karensa and from now onward all those who trust in you will be welcomed into the Royal Palace. Meanwhile, let the battle continue. Now my people must choose whom they will follow and Bellum will try everything in his power to keep them from coming to me. My friends, this is where the real conflict starts."

Veritan lifted high the golden sword of truth and a great and mightly call to arms resounded around the Hall and was carried to the ends of the Earth.

ISBN 1 85999 463 6